The
Tear Collector

ALSO BY PATRICK JONES

Things Change
Nailed
Chasing Tail Lights
Cheated
Stolen Car

The
Tear Collector

. . . .

Patrick Jones

. . . .

WALKER & COMPANY

New York

To Laura and Kim for their continued support

First published in the United States of America in 2009 by Walker Publishing Company, Inc.
Visit Walker & Company's Web site at www.walkeryoungreaders.com

For information about permission to reproduce selections from this book, write to
Permissions, Walker & Company, 175 Fifth Avenue, New York, New York 10010

Library of Congress Cataloging-in-Publication Data
Jones, Patrick.
The tear collector / Patrick Jones.
p.   cm.
Summary: As one of an ancient line of creatures who gain energy from human tears, seventeen-
year-old Cassandra offers sympathy to anyone at her school or the hospital where she works, but
she yearns to be fully human for the boy she loves, even if it means letting her family down.
ISBN-13: 978-0-8027-8710-1 • ISBN-10: 0-8027-8710-X (hardcover)
[1. Supernatural—Fiction. 2. Sympathy—Fiction. 3. High schools—Fiction. 4. Schools—Fiction.
5. Identity—Fiction. 6. Family life—Michigan—Fiction. 7. Michigan—Fiction.] I. Title.
PZ7.J7242Ted 2009   [Fic]—dc22   2008055868

Book design by Nicole Gastonguay
Typeset by Westchester Book Composition
Printed in the U.S.A. by Quebecor World Fairfield
2 4 6 8 10 9 7 5 3

ACKNOWLEDGMENTS

The core story of *The Tear Collector* came to me driving from Fort Wayne IN to Flint MI. During those three hours in March 2008, the basic elements of the book emerged. I immediately began testing the idea out "on the road" during school visits in Michigan, Illinois, and Wisconsin, to great response. So, thanks to all those students in schools from spring 2008 who asked questions or commented on the basic idea. In particular, a special thanks to teens I met on the road who read the book in manuscript. Without the input, ideas, and energy of Gabby Anderson, Zac Fink, Larissa Grundmanis, Katie Jo Jerzak, Tara Kane, Heajin Kim, Andi Lemons, Tiana McAllister, Kelly McCarten, and Lauren Morris, there'd be no *Tear Collector*. A special thank-you to Elizabeth Straub and Sara Misgen from the YA Galley group in St. Paul MN, who showed off their reviewing skills with detailed comments on the manuscript.

The poem "I hurt, hurt, hurt" in Chapter 17 was written by Andi Lemons.

A special thanks to Dr. Ann Albrecht from Tarleton State University in Texas for information on school counselors. As always, thanks to Amy Alessio and Patricia Taylor for reading and commenting on an early draft, and Erica Klein for her support for two decades.

But mostly, thanks to the nameless teen girl at the Allen County Public Library in Fort Wayne IN who, when asked by a librarian if she'd like to read my novel *Things Change*, answered, "No. I only read vampire books." It was that anonymous Hoosier girl—and the music of Van Morrison—that inspired me to cry these Tears.

The law of conservation of energy
states that *energy cannot be created or destroyed*;
it can only be changed from one form to another.

Other animals howl when they are in distress,
but only humans weep tears of sorrow—or joy.
—Chip Walter, "Why Do We Cry?"
Scientific American, November 2006

Jesus wept.
—John 11:35

NEWS REPORT #1

Michigan State Police have issued an AMBER Alert for eleven-year-old Robert Sanders. Sanders, a fifth-grade student at Bay City Elementary, was last seen leaving school on March 4. According to witnesses, he was walking home alone. Law enforcement officials are on the lookout for a black Ford van seen in the area earlier in the day.

CHAPTER I

FRIDAY, MARCH 6

*A*re you crying?" I ask as I tap on the driver's side window of the white Chevy Impala. Inside the familiar car, I see the unfamiliar sight of my best friend, Robyn Berry, crying.

"Robyn, it's Cassandra," I say. It's a wonder she can see or hear; she's drowning in tears. She takes a second to collect herself, then opens the window. With her perfect makeup smeared, it's as if she's wearing a monster mask instead of her always-smiling cheerleader face.

"Hey, Cass," she forces out through sniffles.

"Let me in," I say, gently enough so she knows I care; hard enough to make it happen.

Robyn clicks the lock, and I walk over to take my usual seat next to her.

"Are you okay? Why didn't you call?" I ask as I climb in. It's odd to see Robyn without her silver phone in her hand or white buds in her ears; both are almost part of her.

She doesn't answer as I sit down, then lean close to her. I offer a sip from my water bottle, but she passes. I take a big slurp, parched from a hard hour of swimming, thanks to Coach Abraham opening up the pool after school. After a quick stop to print something at the library, I was on my way home when I saw Robyn's car at the back of the school parking lot.

"It's okay to cry, Robyn," I say softly, encouraging another emotional outburst. She listens, letting loose a torrent of tears. I slip off my jacket—actually my soon-to-be-ex-boyfriend Cody's varsity jacket—then pull her close, letting her tears fall on my bare left shoulder. I'm wearing a simple gray tank top set off by the tie-dyed bandanna holding back my long multi-colored hair. My hair is like my life: mostly dark, but with a few streaks of light and color added in.

I don't say anything; instead, I let her cathartic tears soak into my skin. After a few minutes, she pulls herself together and retreats toward her side of the car. Lapeer High School runs on rumors, and someone seeing two girls hugging in a car is inviting gossip, lies, and drama. Who is and isn't preg-nant, gay, bi, or hooking up keeps the rumor tides ebbing and flowing.

"Thanks, Cass," she says, then sniffs to signal an end to this round of eye rain.

"Like that Beatles song says, you get by with a little help from your friends," I tease. I turned Robyn on to the Beatles, while she's always trying to get me to listen to the latest big thing. That's why Robyn and I are such good friends; we make up for each other's deficiencies.

She still doesn't say anything, so I ask, "What's wrong?"

"Everything," she answers, which sets off a few more drops of liquid despair.

"Something with Becca?"

"No, she's fine," she says, even as her brief nervous laughter dissolves into almost mandatory tears. Becca is Robyn's younger sister. She's eight and she has cancer, so she probably won't turn nine.

"She's a fighter," I say. Robyn forces a smile; there's a lot of faking in the face of death.

Becca's the glue that holds together our friendship. I didn't know Robyn well until last spring, when I learned about her sister through my volunteer work at the hospital. I knew Robyn would need a friend like me who could comfort her rather than all those selfish hanger-on types who feed off her, like Brittney and Kelsey. Like me, Robyn's popular. She cruises easily among everyone, but as a cheerleader, she's got her main crew. I'm all over, like a sponge soaking up friends from all cliques. But I'm always there for Robyn, to listen to her problems or babysit Becca so Robyn can hang with her superficial friends. She's again learning—as have others at Lapeer High since ninth grade—that I'm the soft shoulder that anyone can cry on during hard times.

"Craig dumped me," she says, each word pulled out of her with great pain like a tooth extraction. He's the perfect jock boy for the cheerleader Robyn. Craig's just like her: attractive, outgoing, and admired. Robyn would be popular without Craig, but he's the icing on her cake. They're not just students; they're stars, but Robyn's the falling one. I'm here to catch her.

"Robyn, I'm so sorry," I say, trying not to stare at the small photo of the once-happy couple hanging from the Impala's rearview mirror. Like that mirror, the photo reflects the past.

"I don't want your pity," she says. "I don't want to be pitiful."

"Why would he do that?"

"Kelsey told me he was cheating. He denied it, we fought, then he ended it. He said we were over," she says. "Craig is the center of my world. If he's gone, then it all falls apart."

"I'd heard rumors too," I mumble. She mouths the word "what" as if she doesn't have enough energy to produce any sounds other than sobbing. "It was true. He was cheating on you."

"Tell me what you know." She's pleading now.

"I heard it was Brittney," I whisper, since that's the tone for spreading a rumor. While I've got experience breaking hearts—as cute but clueless Cody's soon to learn—I couldn't tell Robyn what I'd heard. It is one thing to watch someone suffer; it is another to be the direct cause.

"How could she do that?" Robyn asks. "She's one of my best friends."

I don't correct her. At school, Robyn mostly hangs out

with Brittney, but it's different away from Lapeer High. From babysitting her sister to eating dinner with her family, I mean more to Robyn than Brittney does. Brittney's all smiles and surface. Brittney clings to Robyn's spotlight and shadow while I'm the drain for the despair and doubt that Robyn hides.

"How could Craig dump me for her?" Her wet eyes stare into mine, but the question isn't aimed at me. It's like she's asking a higher power to explain the unfairness of the universe.

"She's supposed to be your friend," I say.

"How could he?" she mumbles. "How could she?"

"I'm your true friend, not Brittney. Have faith in me," I say, then move closer. I finger the three necklaces pressing against my skin and that signify my beliefs. Except when I swim or take a quick shower, I'm never without my trinity of faith: a peace-sign button on a hemp string, a gold crucifix hanging from a gold chain, and a silver necklace with a crystal teardrop charm.

"Craig said he loved me," she says while avoiding my sympathetic eyes. She doesn't know that's all I offer: sympathy. I have no empathy for her, or for anyone else suffering from a broken heart. I can no more understand love than a blind person can comprehend color.

"I guess he lied," I say.

"How could he not want me?" Robyn asks the universe through me. She's struggling with her words like a rookie actor onstage. Words of rejection and failure are new to Robyn.

"Everybody knows you're wonderful and he's a jerk," I remind her.

"Once people hear, they'll be laughing at me," she says. "People want me to fail."

"Come on, Robyn, nobody will laugh at you," I say. "Everybody loves you."

"No, people hate me, I know it," she says with a hiss. "They're jealous."

"Don't say that," I say, but I don't deny it. People *are* jealous of her outwardly perfect life, including me. Envy, anger, and fear are the only emotions I feel deeply; others I only fake. Yet, even as I see Robyn suffer because of love, I know it's the one emotion I want for myself.

"It's not my fault I'm pretty," she says. With her blond hair, blue eyes, and faultless figure, every straight guy wants her. Yet because she's nice and never stuck-up, most girls envy her, but none outwardly hate her. "I didn't ask to be popular."

"I know, it is just who you are," I say. She's popular because she's pretty and good at talking to people; I'm popular because I'm pretty enough and great at listening to people.

"I work hard in school and everything else," Robyn says through more tears. The breakup has broken down her self-control. "I have to be the best. It's my nature."

"Do you want me to drive you home?" I ask, very tentatively. As one of the few juniors at Lapeer High School without a car, my time behind the wheel is limited. I have a license indicating Michigan trusts me to drive, but I have a mom who doesn't share the state's faith.

"I don't want to go home," Robyn says, still whispering like there's no energy left in her body to speak. "I can't take another thing. Everybody there wants so much of me."

"I understand," I say. While I identify with family obligations, it's not the pressure to succeed that Robyn feels from her engineer dad and lawyer mom. Her parents want their daughter to succeed, but what Robyn hears, I think, is she isn't allowed to fail. Add in cheerleading, honors classes, and being the perky popular girl, and it's a mix that would break most normal human beings.

"And I can't tell anyone how hard it all is."

"You can tell me," I say, then remind her of my mantra. "You can trust me."

"I want to be able to tell my parents that it's all too much. With Becca, they have so much to worry about," she says, and the tears start to fall again. "Sometimes I think it would be better if I were dead."

I don't respond; instead, I let more drops soak into my shoulder and I feel a rush from the energy in the tears, probably the way an addict feels getting his fix from his drug of choice.

When I'm so full that I'm almost disoriented, I take a monogrammed white linen handkerchief from my back pocket. I gently transfer the tears from her face to this old-fashioned yet invaluable family heirloom. I pull her close, so she can't see the smile forming on my face as a waterfall of tears continues to cascade from her eyes. Robyn needs to cry, but what she doesn't know—and nobody outside of my family could imagine—is that I need her to cry even more. Just as a vampire needs to suck blood to live, I need to collect tears in order to survive.

CHAPTER 2

SATURDAY, MARCH 7

*C*an I help you?"

"I'm looking for the chaplain's office," the older man responds to my query in a dazed voice. He's shell-shocked, standing in the safe bright hallways of Lapeer Regional Medical Center. It's a look of loss: lost not in the building but in his grief. I see that look a lot here.

I walk him over to the map on the wall, then give directions. He tries to force a smile, but I can tell it's too hard. "Happy to help," I say as he walks away. Other than in the maternity ward, hospitals don't birth many smiles. This is a place of death, sickness, and sorrow.

I've been a volunteer at the hospital since we moved to Lapeer. Over the past two-plus years, I've worked every Saturday unless I've had a swim meet, church, or family obligation. On Sundays, I do double shifts after Mass. During the summer, I put in even more hours. Now that swimming season is over, I can volunteer two more nights a week. When I started, like all new volunteers, I did boring stuff and didn't interact with patients or families. Now the staff trusts me. They've seen how good I am at comforting people, so they bend the rules. I spend most of my time up in Pediatrics. It was there that I found out about Robyn's terminally ill sister, Becca.

I walk back to organize my cart when I hear, "I heard you're breaking up with Cody."

I turn to see Kelsey, another volunteer adorned in the standard white button-down blouse and black dress pants of the hospital volunteer uniform. Like me, Kelsey's a junior and a swimmer. We also share the same history class, Robyn's friendship, and another common experience. She's dating Tyler Adams, one of my ex-boyfriends, so we're natural enemies. "Who told you that?" I ask.

"Everybody knows," she snaps back.

"It doesn't involve you," I counter, but don't deny it. For once, this bit of backstabbing gossip isn't a lie. Now I understand why Cody's been texting me like crazy all day. I won't text or call him back. Cody knows my rules: breakups, like makeouts, must occur in person. If he wants to fight or fool around, he needs to let me stare into his dark brown eyes.

"Why do you care?" I ask, then start to walk away.

"How many hearts do you plan on breaking?" Kelsey asks, all sarcastic.

"Tyler's only going out with you because you remind him

of me," I fire back. I hate angry conflicts; I have enough of them at home. I don't need Kelsey sapping my strength.

"You wish," she replies, but without much confidence.

"You know I'm right," I say, then start again to walk away. In some ways, looking at Kelsey is like looking in a mirror. We're the same medium height with the similar lean-but-mean female swimmer body type. I'm thinner and smaller everyplace, but I have no trouble getting attention. Kelsey sports a short blond hairdo, but I let my locks grow long so my tricolored hair (natural black tinted with red and yellow) tickles my exposed shoulders. With Kelsey's tight clothes turning her cleavage into an eye magnet, no boy's looking at her hair anyway.

"You're so weird," she says, the all-purpose high school put-down.

I sigh, then turn again to face her. "And you're so normal. Tyler will tire of you soon enough. He'll be afraid the dullness will wear off on him."

She leans in toward me, then whispers, "Well, unlike Cody, at least Tyler gets off."

"Whatever," I say, and sigh. She's guessing, which accounts for most gossip. Rumors are lies that sometimes turn out to be true. I think that's what happened with Robyn and Craig. The word was Craig hooked up with Brittney. So, maybe they figured they might as well act on it. I don't know, just like I don't know who started the rumor, but I do know that Kelsey spread it like the plague.

"What did Tyler tell you about me?" I whisper back, then

take a sip from my water bottle. All these heated words are drying out my mouth.

"You're a virgin," Kelsey says, and I breathe a sigh of relief if that's all he said.

I sigh loudly, then announce, "It's none of your business."

She laughs, which draws unwanted attention from the nurses' station. I want to get away from Kelsey and get back to work. I couldn't bear to get fired; this volunteer job sustains me.

"Cassandra, at Lapeer, everything is everybody's business," she says, reminding me of the hard truth of high school. I know I have a reputation as a heartbreaker, but it hasn't hurt me yet. I've broken up with Cody before, but we bounced right back. There was shouting (me), followed by tears (him). We'd make up, make out, and break up again. But this is probably Cody's last ride. Like Tyler, he'll find somebody else. So will I. I always do, which is why I'm always looking.

"I have things to do, don't you?" I snap, but Kelsey's not moving.

"I don't know how you can work here."

"What do you mean?" I ask her, then pull out some lip balm. She's really drying me out.

"The doctors here pledge to do no harm, but that's all you do," she says, and hisses.

"I'm here to help people, not hurt them."

"Don't be all like that," she counters. "I see through your helpful-friend act."

"What are you talking about?"

"Pretending like you care about anyone that is hurting," she says. "Like how you've used Becca to become Robyn's best friend over Brittney and me. It makes me sick."

"No, it makes you jealous," I snap back instead of admitting she's right. With my great-grandmother Veronica's failing health and her needing my help, it's like this past year I've been on sympathy steroids. My first two years at Lapeer, I offered my shoulder only to friends, but this junior year, I'm looking for anyone who is hurt. Kelsey's right; I'm a heartache whore.

"Tyler is so cool, why did you hurt him?" she asks. There's anger in her eyes, but there's no regret in mine. "Now you're gonna do the same to Cody. What's wrong with you?"

"Kelsey, you're not my family and you're not my friend. I don't answer to you."

"Before Tyler, there were like six others. After Cody, do you already have someone lined up?" she asks. "Maybe you're the one stealing Craig away from Robyn."

"My name isn't Burnt Knees. I mean Brittney." I point to my name tag, then fake a smile. Burnt Knees is a nickname that someone bestowed upon Brittney and then spread around school.

"You're such a bitch," Kelsey says with a hiss. "I don't know why Robyn stays friends with you."

"At least I'm Robyn's friend," I snap. "You're only friends with her because of Brittney. And, just in case you haven't noticed, you're not even Brittney's friend either."

"What do you mean?" she asks, looking confused.

"You're not her friend; you're her toady!" I'm angry not so much at Kelsey, but at how Brittney uses her. "No matter how much makeup you use, your nose is still gonna be brown."

She answers by staring me down, but blinks as I ask, "Do you think any of this matters?"

"What are you talking about?"

"Kelsey, look around on this floor. Go up to the burn unit. Or to the ICU. Come with me to Pediatrics. Then you'll understand what I mean," I tell her. "These people are in real pain with life-and-death situations, and you're talking about boyfriends and breakups."

"Don't go acting all mature on me," is her weak counter.

"You think the sick kids up there cry as much as people at school do about lame high school drama?" I ask, then answer, "They don't. It is too bad that Tyler was upset and Cody will feel hurt. But compared to people here, their trivial pain doesn't even begin to match up."

To prove my point, I quickly scan the hallway. We're just in a regular unit, but I quickly home in on the sound, smell, and even the taste. I dismiss Kelsey with a glare, then walk toward a room near the end of the hall. I take a deep breath, then ask, "Are you okay?"

The woman—maybe forty or fifty—turns around. She's nicely dressed, plenty of jewelry, but no makeup. She knows better than to apply makeup that will only wash away. I saw

her here last week. It's her mother lying in the bed, hooked up
to tubes pushing life-giving liquid through her veins. "I'm just
tired," she replies in a tone that shows speaking to a stranger is
almost more energy than she can spare. I break the rules and
hug her softly as a few of her tears fall onto me, then we walk
into the room. I help sit her down in a blue chair and the grief
swallows her like an ocean. The mom is dying, the daughter is
crying, and I'm here to help.

The rest of my shift goes well. I avoid Kelsey and encounter
more family members that I can comfort. I'm not sure why
Kelsey even volunteers here. She must have some other motive.
The other girls—like Amanda, who sometimes gives me a ride
home—seem more the type. Like me, they want to help people
or learn more about medicine. Maybe Kelsey's just trying to
meet a medical student. Everybody has good intentions, I suppose, but all with strings attached.

That thought is on my mind as Cody arrives. The SUV
shakes with booming bass. He parks his dad's black SUV in
the handicapped zone, then walks toward the front door. He's
dressed for Saturday night, with new green shades, blue Hollister hoodie, and fake surfer-boy tan. Cody thinks he's cool, and
he is when he's with Tyler and Craig, but on his own, he's just
another guy who tries too hard. But he says he loves me, and
that's enough for now. I sigh, and then get a head start on the
night's activities by unbuttoning the top button of my blouse.

. . .

"What do you know about Craig and Brittney?" I ask Cody, my head across his chest.

"What?" he mumbles. He's satisfied, half asleep; I'm wide-awake and full of energy. It's midnight, and we're lying fully clothed in front of the sofa. Upstairs, I hear Cody's parents going about their adult business; down here, I've performed my girlfriend duties for their son.

"You're good friends with Craig, right?" I ask.

"I'm tight with C-Dawg," Cody says, and I'm trying not to laugh. Nothing in Cody's spoiled suburban life justifies his ripped-off rap lexicon.

"Is it true about Craig and Brittney?" I ask.

"It's Robyn's own fault," he says, then laughs. "She should've lived up to her name."

"What do you mean?" I ask, but I have a good idea. While Robyn and I don't talk much about sex—and nowhere near as much as guys do—she confessed her inexperience and reluctance despite her love for Craig. Like me, she's a "virgin." Unlike me, there's no qualification to that word.

"Robyn wouldn't swallow Craig's worm!" Cody laughs so loud, he starts coughing.

I fake a laugh, which isn't all I need to fake with Cody, since he's all about Cody. It just gives me another reason to break up with him. There are so many, it will be hard to choose just one. He's had his fun. He's fallen in love with me, and very soon, it'll be time for me to move on.

"We should totally roll to his crib," Cody says through

another yawn. I can't imagine why Cody would be tired. He's in between sports seasons, he doesn't work or volunteer, and from what I know about his grades, he doesn't study. He brags about how he doesn't do anything around the house. Like the Brittneys of the world, Cody's just somebody who takes.

"I gotta go. I have church in the morning," I say, then fake a yawn. Being with Craig and Brittney would be raw betrayal. Seeing Craig and Cody play video games is rawer boredom.

"You wanna hang out after, catch a movie or come over here?" he asks.

I swallow a sigh, then say, "I have other things to do."

"You mean other *guys* to do," Cody says sharply. He doesn't handle even the tiniest rejection well. Good-looking guys like Cody are so used to getting their way that any obstacle sinks their self-esteem. Cody types think they can walk on water, yet they drown so easily.

I raise my head off his shoulder and stare into his brown eyes. "Cody, that's a lie."

"That's not what Kelsey told me," he says, sitting up straight.

"Don't believe everything you hear, especially from Kelsey," I say.

"That's harsh," Cody says, then makes the universal cat-fight sound.

I fake another laugh, then say, "Besides, when Kelsey's lips move, it's Brittney talking."

"You straight with me?" he asks, trying to seem so strong, but without his sports uniform, he doesn't look or act tough. He breaks just like a little boy.

"Cody, don't worry about that," I whisper into his ear. "Don't worry about anything."

"It's just that—," he starts, then stops.

I wipe my hands near his not-yet-crying eyes, then say, "I love you, Cody." As desired, Cody's eyes start to well with tears of joy. Joyful tears are not as powerful, but just as welcome.

"I know it, Shawty," he says, then smiles.

"I won't hurt you," I reassure him, then put my head back on his chest. I know both the things I just told him are lies, but they're the words that he wants to hear. I might as well let Cody be happy for the rest of the time we're together. I might not be human, but that doesn't mean I'm a monster.

CHAPTER 3

SUNDAY, MARCH 8

How's Veronica?"

"You're late," is my mom's answer to my query about my great-grandmother.

"I did an extra Sunday shift at the hospital," I say, which I know gives me a free pass. Duty trumps everything in this house. Maybe that's why I spent the morning at church, the afternoon at the hospital, and the evening at a Starbucks listening to my theater pal, Michael, pour out all his problems. I'm always surrounded by people, and yet I'm all alone in the world.

"Always an excuse," Mom says.

"If you'd let me drive, I wouldn't have to wait on friends," I remind her. Although calling the girl—Amanda—who often gives me rides home a "friend" stretches that word to the limit. Amanda and I share the same place at the same time, but nothing else. It's a connection built on convenience and coincidence; I know a lot about those relationships in high school.

"She's asking for you," is Mom's sidestepping response.

She's sitting at the kitchen table drinking bottled water. Like everyone in my family, Mom lives, dresses, and consumes simply, acting out her beliefs in her daily life. She runs the local Red Cross. Anytime there's a trauma or tragedy, from fire to flood and anything in between, Mom finds herself in the middle.

"Have you dealt with *that boy* yet?" Mom asks. Her term "that boy" refers to every boy I've dated in high school. She's never met one or even bothered to learn their names.

"Cody," I remind her. "And, no, I haven't."

"You know my rules," Mom says, sipping water like fine wine.

"I'll take care of it," I say.

"I want this handled before the reunion next month," Mom says. I nod in obedience.

"Veronica's *still* waiting," Mom says, then points upstairs like I'm a dog. That is all I do: obey. We move around the country, but for me, nothing changes. I just go where I'm kicked.

"Okay, I'll see her," I say, but first I head toward my room. It's hard to call it "my room," considering how often we move. I know this house is rented, and in a few years, someone else will hang their posters on these walls. Still, I can't be without the Beatles watching over me. From my first listen to songs like "Across the Universe" and "Let It Be," I was hooked by the majestic sound and, for me, unattainable emotion within their words and music. Yet, mostly it's envy of their power to move people to tears. They're my beautiful obsession.

I toss my/Cody's coat on the bed and then drop my book

bag on the floor with a *thud*. Like Robyn, I take a few honors courses, and part of the honor seems to be building bigger muscles carrying the weight of the texts. I turn the humidifier up to high and pull out a fresh bottle of moisturizer I'll apply after a swift shower. On top of the moisturizer, I'll add a layer of baby oil. This routine is about the only thing to keep my skin from flaking away like a dried-up sponge.

I jump on the computer, check for messages, and hit my favorite sites like a doctor at the hospital making rounds. I pull up a news story from nearby Bay City and print the item. I read the short article, unlock my desk, and then put it in the folder with the other articles I'm collecting. As I'm locking up my desk, I hear Grandmother Maggie call my name through the locked door. Just in yelling my name, she sounds annoyed, disappointed, and concerned. Her ambivalent tone of voice reflects her attitudes toward me better than anything she does or says.

"I'm busy," I snap. Maggie and I get along better than Mom and I, which isn't saying much. We have a secret connection: our shared, if unspoken, impatience with our mothers.

"Veronica's asking for you," she says, and I stifle both a laugh and a frown. My great-grandmother Veronica never asks for anything; she only expects and demands.

"Five minutes," I huff out, then click off the screen. The news will wait; the old can't.

"Now," Maggie barks. As I think of Veronica waiting for me, I know there's only one thing to do, since I can't deny duty; I choose petty defiance. I turn off the computer while turning on my phone. Robyn doesn't pick up her cell, so I call her at home. Her mother answers.

"Hello," she says.

"Hey, Mrs. Berry, is Robyn there?" I ask.

"I'm sorry, Cassandra, she's already asleep," she says in a motherly tone. "I don't think she's feeling well. Might be the flu. You can't be too careful."

"Can you tell her I called?"

"Sure. Cassandra, as long as I have you, I need to ask you something," she says. I'm trying to focus on Robyn's mother's words as my grandmother bangs on the door, loudly.

"John and I have our twentieth anniversary coming up on April ninth," she starts. "We'd like you to babysit Becca for us that night, if you don't have other plans."

"I'm always happy to be there for Becca," I say, knowing Cody's long gone by then.

"Thanks. I'd have Robyn do it," she says, then pauses. "But she and Craig are the ones taking us to dinner. Isn't that sweet of them? They are just the sweetest kids and cutest couple."

I pause. The knock at the door echoes the loud pounding in my head. I'm just beginning to understand how difficult this breakup is for Robyn. In this house, my breakups get greeted with celebration. In Robyn's house, it will be devastation. I wonder how long Robyn can keep it a secret. That's another area where I could be of great support.

"Are you there?" Mrs. Berry asks.

"Sure, sorry, just checking my schedule," I lie. "Of course I can do it."

"Thanks. You're such a help to us and a good friend to my girls," she says. "I'll tell Robyn you called. It might make her feel better. I know Becca always feels better after you visit."

"Thanks," I reply, then say my good-byes. I know there's nothing that will make Robyn feel any better anytime in the future. When we spoke yesterday, that was all she talked about: the Beatles song "Yesterday." She said how the line in the song "there's a shadow hanging over me" described her life. When she tells her parents, those shadows are sure to grow darker.

I'm surprised to find Maggie still standing by the door when I finally emerge from my room. We both still have our uniforms on: mine is from the hospital; hers is from Avalon Convalescence Care, this nursing home where she's head nurse. In the summer, I volunteer there too. I don't like being there, but I don't have a choice. No wonder I relate so well to the patients.

"Cassandra, you can't act this way," Maggie says. "Especially at the reunion."

"I don't want to go," I say. In four weeks is our family reunion. I hate it, but I do like seeing my cousins Lillith and Mara, as well as almost all of the male cousins, except Alexei. Yet this year, I dread it worse than ever. That coming weekend, not "yesterday," is the shadow hanging over me. Anytime I speak of missing it, Maggie tells me there is no choice. Those who refuse to attend or break family rules, like my cousin Siobhan, become exiles forever.

"Your cousin Alexei will be there," Maggie says, sounding enthusiastic.

"I know," I mumble, keeping hidden all I know about him. But I also know my duty to my family and what I'm expected to do. Maggie, even more than Veronica, raves about him.

"Alexei just turned seventeen recently too," she says. "You could learn a lot from him."

I think of all the evidence that contradicts her, but I don't bother to say anything. "What do you mean?"

"He understands family and duty," she says. "He's not self-ish, like you're becoming."

"Selfish?" I wonder if my eyes are popping out of my head. I am many things, but selfish isn't one of them. "I do whatever I'm asked. I've sacrificed a normal life for this family."

Maggie stares me down, "You have a duty to family. Some of the things you do—"

"I do those things for us, not for me."

"No, you are selfish," she intones. "Our existence owes itself to sacrifice."

"Then when are any of you going to sacrifice for me?" I ask, but don't give her time to respond. "You all ask so much and I get nothing in return. When do you do anything for me?"

"You mean other than this roof over your head?" Maggie replies.

"Why can't it be one roof? Why do we keep moving? Why do I need to go out and make new friends all the time? Why do I always make the sacrifices? Why do—," I say, then stop dead. And Grandma Maggie looks as if she's about to stop breathing. I start to walk away.

"Turn around!" she yells, but I ignore her, and I hope we both can ignore what occurred: I almost weep, like any other teenage girl. But I consume tears; I don't release them.

I knock on Veronica's door, then enter once she grants permission. The lights are off, but a ray of moonlight shines through the window. The long white veil she often wears lies across the end of the bed. It must be a trick of the light, but her dry, scaly skin looks as yellow as the moon. Like everyone in this house, she's thin with little body fat. None of us can stand the cold Michigan climate, but Veronica moved us here from New Orleans, just as she moved us from NYC to New Orleans. She's always looking for opportunity, but I'm not sure what she sees in Lapeer. It's east of Flint—once the most dangerous city in the United States—and people here seem like everybody else. Whatever the reason, Veronica hasn't shared it with anyone.

Veronica's lying in bed, where she spends most of her days and nights anymore. It is rare that she leaves the house. On the nightstand are various bottles and vials filled with liquids to prevent her from dehydrating. Her voice is weak. I lean in close and still must strain to hear her.

"How was the hospital?" she whispers, but her soft voice still speaks volumes. The question is meant to challenge me, and there's no right answer. Unlike me, everything out of Veronica's mouth is judgmental. She builds me up only to knock me down and put me in my place. That place is medical school. Veronica worked as a hospice nurse, guiding people along the final steps of life, but she wants me to become a life-saving doctor. Everything that weighs me down—the Honors Biology class, the hospital job, and the peer counseling service at school—is because of her expectations. Now homebound and weak, she demands even more from me.

"Okay," I mumble. After this past weekend with Robyn, Kelsey, and moving closer to breaking Cody's heart, I feel as tired and worn down as she looks.

She takes a couple of deep breaths. Talking with Veronica is like conversing on a cell phone with a bad connection; it is full of long moments of silence. And plenty of interrupting: always her, never me. "You're late," she says, sounding exactly like my mother. They're twins separated by a generation, much like Grandma Maggie and me. "I want to hear about that girl Robyn."

I briefly recap Robyn's rumor-inspired heart-wrecking breakup. Veronica sits up a little more in bed, puts her old dry hand on my shoulder, then says, "You know what you must do."

"I know." The only four-letter word that matters is *must*. Not *want*, not *love*. But *must*.

"We depend on you, Cassandra," she reminds me for the

millionth time. Veronica's admonishments consistently remind me of my obligations and her infinite expectations.

"I saw that woman with the dying mother again before I left the hospital," I say to change the subject. Robyn isn't something I want to think about; I want to talk about her even less.

"You did good," she says softly. In the space between those words, however, I think what she's really saying is "You did good, *but not good enough.*"

"You feeling any better today?" I ask. Awaiting her answer, I'm overcome by my ambivalence toward Veronica. I fear her pronouncements, yet I envy her special gifts. But mostly I'm angry at how her weakness sucks the life out of the rest of us. I sense this in many people who visit their loved ones in the hospital. They love them and want them well, but the strain in the eyes shows another truth: they resent the ill. While Robyn would never say it—as it might cause the halo to fall from around her golden-haired head—she resents Becca. She resents all the attention that Becca sucks up from everyone; death and illness are time vacuums.

"Cassandra, child, you *always* make me feel better," she says, but, like everything with Veronica, words have two meanings. "Always" isn't a compliment, it is an expectation.

I suck it up and give her the obligatory embrace, then start to leave.

"You're holding back," she whispers. Her five senses are failing; her sixth remains strong. I could never, ever lie to Veronica, but of late, I don't tell her the whole truth of my life.

I don't deny it; instead, I lean toward her. Up close, I notice just how weak she really is. I take the handkerchief out of my back pocket. I gently rub my fingers over the monogram with Veronica's initials, then dip the tip of it in a small bowl of liquid near her bed. Her skin is almost translucent; the blue veins look like rivers about to burst their banks. I squeeze the handkerchief like a sponge and let the fluid run down her satisfied and saturated face onto her bare shoulders.

NEWS REPORT #2

Michigan State Police reported that Robert Sanders, a fifth-grade student at Bay City Elementary missing since March 4, has been found. Sanders disappeared after school and was returned to the school's playground sometime early Sunday morning. At this point, police are releasing few other details, except that the search continues for a black Ford van seen in the area earlier in the day. One source reported that the abduction seemed "abnormal," as the motive, while unclear, does not seem to have involved ransom or sexual assault.

CHAPTER 4

MONDAY, MARCH 9

Is everything okay?" I ask, lightly tapping on the marked-up puke green bathroom stall door.

"Leave me alone," an unfamiliar female voice hisses back. For a second, the sobbing sounded like Robyn, but that was wishful thinking on my part. I thought she might come back today, but even though Robyn's strong, she's not that strong. She's probably faking an illness to hide not only the breakup but also her own heartbreak from her parents. She knows how rumors fly around this place. I've yet to hear a hint before school, but by the end of the day, the news could be like a raging river flood. It only takes one person to break the dam of silence.

"Sorry," I say to the girl in the stall, wondering who is inside and how I can help. Between classes, the bathroom's packed with girls texting and talking but few tearing up. I tape on the smudged mirror a flyer about the school's peer counseling service. A couple of girls snicker, but I ignore them. They're smug and happy now, but they'll need someone like me one day.

"I thought you drowned, Swimmer Girl," Cody says, when I finally emerge.

"Only in your love," I say, then kiss him on the cheek. My small hand folds into his, and we start walking together. As we're walking through the crowded halls, Cody acts as if we're the only two people in the world. Six months ago, Cody wanted me, but now he needs me; he loves me. At first when walking together, Cody held me in a headlock, but I cut him off until that behavior stopped. Boys, like most mammals, need training before they're fit for society.

"You wanna roll tonight, Shawty?" he asks. I give him another kiss on the cheek—nothing else is permitted in Lapeer's halls; almost everything else takes place in the school's parking lot after, before, and during school. There are plenty of four-wheel hotels around here.

"Sure." I'm trying not to laugh. We always roll back to the same place: his basement.

"I can't wait," he says, pulling me closer, maybe hoping he can hold me forever. But I know that, like a calendar, Cody's days are numbered. It's just a matter of how, when, and where. He'll get hurt no matter what I say, so I need to plan for the best possible outcome for both of us.

I sneak a full-mouth kiss, sucking on Cody's bottom lip

like a Life Saver, and then turn toward the door. He says good-bye with a kiss on the cheek and a very public smack on my behind. I sigh, then slip in the door as the second bell rings for first period. My last-second arrival draws a frown from Mr. Abraham, our Honors Biology teacher and my mentor.

Mr. Abraham (also known as Mr. A) is not someone I want to disappoint. He's the school's swimming coach, and as our adviser, he helped Robyn, me, and some other girls set up the school's peer counseling program last spring. In class, he's tough but fair. He doesn't lecture so much as lead the discussion. He has a swimmer's body and wears his auburn-just-turning-gray hair short. Half the girls have crushes on him, and a few gay guys do too. His ice blue eyes freeze you in place, and the gentleness of his voice pins you down.

"So, let's talk about the articles I asked you to read," he says after everyone settles. My phone's buzzing. Mr. A's already taken my phone twice this term; the third time means serious trouble. I wait until he turns to write on the board, then I sneak a peek. Cody's calling. I know he's in English class now with Kelsey, so she's spreading her shit, and I'll have to clean it up. I'll hook up with Cody at lunch and erase Kelsey's rumor, his doubts, and his midday desires.

Mr. Abraham turns and looks at the sea of young faces in this class, which started with the second term in January. All these juniors are so bright, yet also totally clueless.

"Who would like to go first?" Mr. A asks. The class looks

like a roller coaster, with almost everyone raising their hands in the air, except for three people, one of whom is me.

Another is Scott Gerard, which isn't so odd, and the other is Samantha Dressen, who is *odd*. Recently broken up after a short but stormy relationship—my sources tell me—*they're* at odds. For weeks she's been staring black eyeliner daggers at Scott the few times he's spoken in class.

Scott transferred in at the start of the term from Powers Catholic. He doesn't talk a lot in class. When he does, half of what he says shows off that he's plenty smart; the other half is smart-ass comments, showing he's got a sense of humor, unlike most people in this class. Because of that, the serious types can't stand him, but I find that mix of shyness and sly comments fascinating. I haven't gotten to know him yet, either because he seems secure or because he's just shy. The truth is probably somewhere in between. His head isn't on his desk—that would call attention—but his silence screams at me. I sense, unlike with Cody, Scott's brain isn't just located between his legs.

Mr. Abraham takes a sip from his thermos, then starts the discussion about intelligent design. It's this movement to teach creation in schools and pretend evolution doesn't exist. Mr. Abraham had us read several articles: half of the articles supported the idea, the other half attacked it. I'm quiet, which is my usual mode. I'll let the normal know-it-alls debate the issue. I'm half listening and half thinking about Cody when I hear a strange sound about five minutes before class ends. Not crying, but the sound people make before they weep. I perk up.

I turn toward the back of the room and notice Samantha is squirming in her seat and raking her black painted nails down her long black sleeves. She's a little overweight, and her layered black Goth attire does a terrible job of hiding it, just like her badly done makeup doesn't really mask her bad skin. I don't know, but I suspect that her every-season long sleeves cover cuts on her arms. I've long found her intriguing, but very hard to get to know. My numerous attempts in the past to befriend her in person and online have failed. Her thick black eyeliner, her jet-black and pink-streaked hair, and her pierced eyebrow announce her interests. She's walking that thin dark line between emo chic and Goth chick. Emos I adore, but Goths, I don't get. One of the beliefs that link them—supernatural beings who live by sucking people's blood—is an utterly absurd notion. What kind of creature could live on the blandness of human blood?

"I think it's wrong," Samantha announces. Everybody looks at her as if they've seen a ghost.

"Miss Dressen, you have something to add?" Mr. Abraham asks, almost stunned she's decided to participate. She's an A student on paper, but an F in the real world.

"It can't be true because there is no God," Samantha announces. Some people giggle, but mostly people act astonished, both by her speaking up in class and the message itself.

"Are you an atheist?" my pal Michael asks in a nonthreatening tone.

"Like any intelligent person would be," Samantha shoots

back. I look up toward Mr. Abraham, but he's content to let the conversation continue. Unlike other teachers, Mr. Abraham isn't just concerned with us memorizing facts; instead, he wants us to think, discuss, and decide.

"Of course there's a God," Mary Nyguen says. It's probably the first time they've ever spoken. There's no natural intersection between the Asian brains and the fringe head cases.

"If so, then which one?" Samantha asks, and then starts pointing around the room, her finger lingering when pointing to Scott. "Your God or yours, or maybe yours?"

It's a class of many creeds—with Asian kids who I think are Buddhist, a couple Muslim kids, and a few Jewish kids—but they all seem united against Samantha. Some of them start to challenge her, but they seem tentative, like lion tamers breaking in a dangerous new cub.

"Why would an intelligent God design a world with so much misery?" Samantha asks, her voice almost cracking as she answers her accusers. "All religion is a lie because no being could be as cruel as God to allow so much suffering and unfairness in the world."

"I'm sorry, but I think you're wrong," Scott says, almost in a whisper. Everybody's waiting for a punch line, but I sense he's serious. Their breakup is breaking out in public.

"Science isn't about what is right or wrong, but what can be proved," Mr. Abraham says.

"Look, I don't want to argue about this," Scott says, a little stronger now. He brushes his long brown hair from in front of his eyes, then says, "I go to church every Sunday and my Catholic youth group every Wednesday night. I believe in God. Nobody is going to convince me otherwise."

"You just don't want to face facts!" Samantha shouts. "God is a crutch for the crippled."

"I have faith in a loving God," Scott replies, as if he is praying aloud. All the hands in the room have gone down, creating the perfect calm for this storm of words and worldviews.

"And all you need is love," I say to an audience of one as I turn to look closer at Scott.

"There is no God. If there ever was, he is dead. And if he's not dead, then with all the pain he's caused, somebody should kill him," Samantha says, as best I can tell. The last few words are swallowed in sniffles as she suffocates the tears forming inside her. I don't see a twisted teen, emo chick, or Goth girl like everyone else; I'm sensing a gusher of hidden hurt.

"God loves you, Samantha," Scott says almost sadly. "God loves all his creatures."

"Creatures of the night," Clark Rogers cracks, and someone else howls like a werewolf.

"Well, this was certainly an interesting debate," Mr. Abraham says. "You see, you can't separate the cold hard truth of science from the hotbed of human emotion. They're linked."

"Can I say something?" I ask as the bell rings. Mr. Abraham

looks skeptical, arching his left eyebrow. He takes another sip from his thermos, then nods in my direction.

"Maybe both Scott and Samantha are right," I say, struggling to be heard over the gathering of books by most and the pushing back of tears by two seemingly pained souls. I said their names loudly hoping to get their attention. "Maybe there's a place between fact and faith."

Mr. Abraham shakes his head in disbelief, as if I were the only other one in the room. I'm not, as both Scott and Samantha remain in their seats like wounded victims on the battlefield. I look at both of them, offering them mercy, but both respond with hard glares. I'm not sure if I've taken the first steps toward two new friends or two new enemies, but either way, both seem perfect sources for me to get my fix of emotional energy.

I head off to my next class. I start walking alone, but that never lasts. After first period, everybody is buzzing about Robyn, and they all think I know something. I gossip for a while, talking a lot but not saying anything, and then slip into a space between two rows of lockers to check messages. There's a new message from Cody, begging me to meet him at lunchtime in his car—a place for makeups, not breakups. There's another message from Robyn, and strangely, one from Craig. Kelsey's wrong; Craig isn't cheating on Robyn with me. But she's right that I did help spread the rumor about Craig and Brittney. Between hookups, makeups, and breakups, at Lapeer

High School there isn't a day without drama turning to trauma turning to tears.

"I gotta go," I say as I put on some more lip balm. I go through a tube a month this time of year, especially in Michigan's dry winter air. I give Cody a good-bye kiss—on the cheek so he's not all weirded out—then leave him satisfied and lighting up a smoke in his car. Lunch is only half over. Like on the basketball court, Cody shoots too quickly for his own good.

I tie Cody's jacket around my waist and jog back toward school. I feel full of energy; energy that's my own, that I don't have to share with anyone.

I try calling Robyn a few more times, but she doesn't pick up. The girl's hurting, and I have to be there for her. I need her back at school and me back in her car. She's got a lot of grief to work through. Breaking up can seem almost like death. There are five stages of grief, but there should be a sixth stage: passing on the hurt to someone who can handle it, someone like me.

I skip eating, instead just drinking from my water bottle, then head to the school library. As with any gathering place, there are plenty of friends in the room, so it takes me a while to choose a seat. I'm about to dive in with some swimmer friends when I see Scott Gerard sitting alone at a round table in the back of the room. I ignore the swimmers and, instead, decide to go fishing.

"That was something in Bio today," I say, sitting down at his table without an invitation.

"I guess," he mumbles, then goes back to reading his book.

"Cassandra, we're in Bio together," I say, lightly, like a joke.

"I know," he says. He mumbles as if his mouth hurts. "I'm sorry. I'm distracted."

"No sweat," I say. "Mind if I sit here?"

He looks at me, then manages a small but nervous smile. "I'd like that."

We read in silence. He reads his biology text; I try to read his secretive green eyes. With long light brown hair that hangs in his face and the start of a mustache and beard, Scott hides his face under a hair mask. He's no Cody in terms of looks, but he does know how to open a book, so that's a plus. After a while, he breaks the silence, and asks, "Who do you think was right?"

"Between you and Samantha?" I ask, and he nods. I pause, take a sip from my water bottle, then say, "Both of you are maybe right. Everything's got an in-between."

"You don't talk much in class either," he says. He's noticed me, just as I've noticed him, but this morning I saw him in a new light. Every flood starts with just one drop of rain.

"I liked how you told Samantha that God loves her." He tugs nervously on the silver cross around his neck as my eyes walk over him. I lean closer to ask, "I wonder who she loves?"

"All Samantha loves is her own misery," he says slowly, then sighs and looks a little ashamed at himself. Unlike me, he doesn't seem to take delight in the sadness of others.

"Ouch," I say, and he laughs. It is more of an "I want to laugh at something you say" chuckle, but it's a start. "So, I guess things are over between the two of you."

"That was wrong. It's just that our breakup is lasting longer than the relationship," he says, then laughs again. Some people laugh at their pain. I normally don't know such people.

"Is there anything I can do to help?" I ask.

He shakes his head, then says, "That's what got me into that mess."

"What do you mean?" I ask, but he pauses, looking unsure. "Scott, you can trust me." I wonder if he knows that "you can trust me" are four words no one should ever believe.

"Well, I was new here and didn't know anybody," he says, then stops again. Scott seems like he wants to talk to me—or maybe just talk—but the words come hard. More than rich and poor, or even black and white, I've noticed a bigger division that runs like a raging uncrossable river in this school. On one side are people like Scott and maybe Samantha, who are—for whatever reason or history—shy, and those people like Cody, Brittney, Robyn, or me, who are not.

"I remember being the new kid," I say. "Was it hard for you?"

"Some people were nice, some people were—"

"Assholes," I say. I curse to let boys to know it's okay to act natural and relaxed around me.

"But still there was a lot of that sitting alone in the cafeteria," he says softly. I'd like to tell him I could relate, but it's not the same for girls. Almost any girl with some self-esteem, a sexy smile, and the right or tight clothes can find boys to sit with at lunch. I always have.

"You're not sitting alone now," I say. He lets his hair fall in front of his face again as if that could hide the blood racing into his blushing cheeks. "So, why Samantha?"

"I'm in Honors English with her, so I know she's smart," he says. He doesn't know that is what fascinates me most about Samantha. Most Goth girls wouldn't be caught alive in honors classes since that's the conformist and normal thing to do. Like me, Samantha seems someone who is at war with her very nature. He sighs, then says, "It seemed like we should get together."

"Really?" I arch a skeptical eyebrow. "No offense, but you don't seem the type to hang out with Samantha." Other than wearing long hair and black Chucks—the choice of emos everywhere—Scott doesn't come off as outside the mainstream. He's pure middle-of-the-river.

When he doesn't respond, I push ahead. "So what happened with Samantha?"

"I thought I could help her," he says, and I sip my water bottle a little faster. "I just want to help people, but it didn't work out. In fact, I think I made things worse."

"I'm sorry to hear that, Scott."

"Everybody's breaking up," he says. Obviously, word about Craig and Robyn is in the bloodstream. "It must be the weather. You know, dark storm clouds in the spring and all."

"Not everybody's breaking up," I say, throwing out more bait. I lip balm up and wait.

"Right, you and Cody," he says, and I bury my smile. He knows a lot about me. "With Robyn and Craig out of the way, you can waltz right into king and queen of the prom."

"I don't think *that's* going to happen," I say with huge exaggeration. He laughs again, which is such an unfamiliar sound. Robyn's always so serious, while Cody's pretty damn dull.

"I'd vote for you," Scott says, then looks down. "Well, if I was going."

"Robyn's available," I say. I'm not as good at matchmaking as I am at heartbreaking. Having Robyn distracted by another boy works against me, but I can't stand to see her hurting. I know better, but I'm too close to Robyn. Maybe Maggie's right about me becoming selfish.

"Right, like *that* is going to happen," he says, then laughs again. I echo the same. We're not the only people talking or laughing in the library, but it seems that way. It's as if the rest of the world is silent and there's only the two of us occupying this round table, this planet. I snap out of it when I hear the loud sound of books knocked off a shelf near us. I look up, and two feet away stands Samantha, her eyes rage red and piercing as she stares at us.

Scott looks like he wants to say something; I suck on my water bottle to silence myself. Samantha knives us both with her eyes, then stomps back the length of the library. We watch as she shuts the door with such force that I'm surprised everyone's not showered in shattering glass.

"Sorry about that!" he says loudly over the growing din. It's as if everyone in the library feels the need to comment on the scene. Scott sighs, then whispers, "Love sure is hard."

"What do you mean?" I ask.

"If love were easy, then it wouldn't hurt," he says. "If it didn't hurt, it wouldn't matter."

I want to say something, except the word "love" means nothing to me. Scott and I fall into silence as the noise level increases. I look at the door and see Kelsey standing with a small group of girls chatting about Samantha's stunt. She stops talking long enough to shoot me a smug smile.

"Again, I'm sorry about that," Scott says as the bell rings, ending the lunch period.

"Don't be sorry, *Scott*, it's not your fault," I say, putting the emphasis all on his name.

"I'm Catholic; I feel guilty about everything," he says, then laughs.

"Me too," I add. The Catholic part is true; the guilt part is a total lie.

"So why didn't you defend religion this morning, Cassandra?" Scott asks, firmly but nicely.

"Because you were doing such a good job," I whisper, then stand up. He smiles through his shyness and gathers his books. It's time for class, so we toss tiny waves before going our separate ways. Like a stone hitting the water, I wonder if today's talk with Scott will result in tiny ripples or a big splash.

CHAPTER 5

THURSDAY, MARCH 12

Promise me, will you please promise me, Robyn?"

"I promise," Robyn replies as her Impala roars out onto the interstate. It's the first time I've seen Robyn in six days. Telling her folks that she's sick, Robyn's missed school every day. Despite my pleas to visit, all we've done is talk on the phone. I finally convinced her to join me this evening. She picked me up after school, and now we're driving down rain-slicked pavement toward the Holly Recreation Area. In a few weeks, my family reunion will take place in one of the parks there. Right now, however, it's just Robyn, me, and the world that's crashed around her.

"Hey, slow down or you'll get a ticket." I notice the speedometer races past eighty.

"What if I do?" she asks. "Just more disappointment for my parents, more drama for me."

"Don't be so hard on yourself." I'm firm yet friendly. "No one expects perfection."

"Oh God, Cass, don't use that peer counseling tone on me," she says.

"You got me," I mutter. Robyn and I were two of the first peer counselors at school, so she sees through my tricks. I don't say anything in return, using silence as bait. Instead, I hand her my iPod, filled with songs carefully selected for this important drive. Robyn hooks up my iPod to the car speakers, then clicks on the music—the magnificent "Let It Be" by the Beatles.

After a while, we pull off I-69 and onto the two-lane road toward the park. Robyn turns down the music but keeps up the speed. "I don't understand why Craig would do this to me."

"Robyn, that's not the way to heal," I tell her.

"What do you mean?"

"You need to stop asking questions that have no answers," I say. "Listen to the song, when you find yourself in times of trouble, just let it be."

"How do I do that?" she asks. "Where do I start?"

"You start healing by crying out the pain," I remind her. For almost a week, we've had the same conversation. She can't move on, it would seem, because she's swimming in circles.

"No. What would people think of me?" she says. "I need to stay strong."

"Don't worry about what people think."

"But I always do," she says, sounding almost sad.

"Robyn, come on, everything is going to be okay after a few months."

"No, it's not. I need this to end. This hurt, this humilia-
tion," she says. "This life!"

She's waiting for me to speak, but I'm drowning in a whirl-
pool of conflicted desires.

"I know, I promise I won't do anything," she says, taking
a big curve at a fast speed.

"Good," I say, and maybe mean it. I'm like a toy top trying
to spin against my rotation.

"I can't go back to school tomorrow," she says. Every
night when we talk, Robyn promises that I'll see her at school
the next day. Every morning so far this week, she's broken that
promise. The old Robyn was perfect and kept every promise; I
don't know about this new Robyn yet. "I know everybody is
going to be laughing at me, especially Brittney."

"Nobody's laughing at you," I reassure her. "You just—"

"But everybody's talking about it, right?" she asks.

"Everybody's on your side," I answer with a slight lie.
Most at school seem sympathetic toward Robyn and angry
at Brittney and Craig. But some girls—with long-hidden
resentment of Robyn now bubbling to the surface—are against
her. The jocks seem divided; half support Craig, while the
other half support Robyn's sudden availability. "It will blow
over and—"

"I'm just so tired." She cuts me off and takes another
curve at well over the recommended speed. "I'm tired of all
the high school drama."

"You're just tired with all that you do. And with Becca, now this—"

Robyn cut me off. "You know what I wish for more than anything?"

"Brittney's head on a plate?" I answer, but there's no lame joke that will put a smile on Robyn's face tonight. Robyn slows down, then pulls the car onto the dirt shoulder. We have a perfect view of a tranquil lake in the twilight hours, yet Robyn's anything but at peace.

"I wish I could trade my life for Becca's," she says. "That's all I want right now."

"Robyn, that's not possible," I say with eyes staring at the floor below me.

"Everybody would be happier," she says. "My parents won't admit it, but I know they'd take the offer in a second. I'm surprised they're not having another kid to mine the marrow."

"That's a terrible thing to say."

"I know, Cass, that's what I'm telling you," she says. "I'm a *terrible* person. I'm supposed to love my sick little sister, but sometimes I resent her so much. I get so *angry* at her."

"You're human," I remind her.

"I'm tired of everyone carrying on about Becca like I don't exist. If we could just trade our lives, everything would be perfect. I'd take my life and by some miracle, transfer it to her."

I go silent. There's so much I want to say to Robyn, but I can't force out the words.

"But there are no miracles, just more heartbreak and more hurt," she says. "I want it to end."

"Craig's just a silly boy, but you're talking murder." I force out these words of mercy.

"I just want the hurt to end," she says. "It's not Craig; it is everything and it is too much."

"Suicide is mass murder, Robyn, because it kills everyone around you," I say. "I know you're not that angry at your parents, at Becca, Craig, or even Brittney. I know you."

She cackles, but that's just the sound of the levee leaking. She starts to cry as she says, "Nobody knows the real me. Can you see the real me?"

I don't answer because she's right. I don't know the real Robyn, and she doesn't know my reality. We're not Best Friends Forever. We're friends doing our best for each other for now.

"I'm *not* the perfect cheerleader. I'm *not* the girl with the cute boyfriend. I'm *not* the girl who loves her dying sister," Robyn says, drowning in self-pity. "I'm nothing."

I wait for her. Finally, she lays her head on my shoulder, soaking it with tears. Against the backdrop of the lake, a small pool of her tears flows over me.

"Craig and I came here," she says once the tears stop. I hand her my handkerchief.

"That is so romantic," I say, thinking about the beauty of

this spot compared to the sofa in Cody's basement or back-seat. Robyn wipes her wet eyes, while I try to wipe away my envy.

"It *was* romantic. Everything is a *was*," she says, her voice barely audible.

"It will be okay," I say. Once again, all I offer is sympathy, not empathy. Romance isn't something that enters into my rela-tionships, which is one reason I'll never end up like Robyn. If you don't feel love—and don't mind being alone—high school becomes very easy.

There's a long pause as Robyn collects herself and returns the moistened handkerchief to me. "I can't live like this. It hurts too much." Her tone is growing more desperate.

"Healing equals tears plus time."

"I don't have any more of either," she says, then sighs. "Cass, would you ask him?"

"Ask who?"

"Would you ask Craig if he'd take me back?"

"I don't know," I say slowly, conflicted between my loyal-ties and selfish motives.

"Tell him—tell him I would do anything to get back with him," she says.

"Don't do that," I say sharply. "Don't sacrifice your *self*."

She laughs, not a real laugh, but rather just a sound to express her shock at my words. "I don't have a self anymore, Cass. When Craig dumped me, he took it with him."

I start to talk, but Robyn exchanges my iPod for hers. She sits back, sighs, and lets "Yesterday" by the Beatles rain over us.

After a while, she pulls back on the road and starts speeding back home. Her phone rings—it's her mom's tone—and she picks up. She doesn't hang up, so I pull out my cell to text Cody. As I'm clicking away, I listen to Robyn trying to act strong, but the longer she talks, the more emotional she becomes. The more emotional she becomes, the faster she drives.

"Slow down," I say as Robyn whips around another turn, with one hand on the wheel.

"One second," she says into the phone, then turns to me. "It's okay."

"We see people DOA in the hospital due to auto accidents," I tell her, speaking slowly so she soaks in my words. "One minute they're driving and living; a minute later they're dead."

"No way I'll ever have an accident," she says. "Don't you know my life is perfect?"

Before I can answer, she's back on the phone with her mom. She's not talking about her situation; she's talking about Becca's next chemo. I end my text to Cody and turn the mirror to apply some makeup for when I see him tonight. Robyn finishes the call, then turns the mirror back toward her. From the mirror hangs a picture of Craig and Robyn from the Valentine's dance. She crumples the picture, opens the window, and tosses it into the wind. She looks at me and says, "I wish someone would just throw me away, put me out of my misery."

I turn to see her mask of tears. I know what I want to say; I know what I must not say. The battle rages within as from some place deep and mysterious inside of me the words *"Please don't cry"* move to the tip of my tongue. I sigh, swallow the words, and Robyn's tears roll on.

"It's a sin," I remind her. Like me, Robyn's Catholic. "Suicide is a sin."

"And I wouldn't want to commit a sin," she says. "That worked out so well with Craig."

I don't say anything about the off-limits subject. Robyn drops to her knees only to pray; Brittney earned her nickname Burnt Knees for good reasons.

"I have to be pure and perfect," she says, pushing down even more on the accelerator.

"You have to be who you are," I say. "You can't deny your nature."

"No, I don't," she counters. "I don't have to be anything. I'm nothing."

"Please, Robyn, stop talking this way," I say, making my very words a lie. You can deny your nature, but only at the risk of losing everything. That's my cousin Siobhan's story.

Robyn stops talking. I make a few attempts, but she's not responding. Driving over the gray pavement, she's living on an emotional fault line. By the time she drops me at my house, it is as if she's flatlined. Robyn's like some movie zombie: not dead but not human.

She doesn't know it, of course, but she's just like me now—not human, but not a classic horror movie vampire either. I'm more of a succubus that maintains a human form to get along in the world but is void of so much of what makes a person human—such as the ability to love. Robyn's lost love for now and I envy her, because I've never felt it and never will. Like animals, my family survives by instinct and the most elemental emotions. We leave the complex emotions to humans and soak up their suffering into our skin to survive. If we'd have emotions, we'd lose all our energy. Instead, we sense sorrow the way vultures and jackals home in on dying animals. The rules of our family prohibit us from directly causing sorrow; instead, we make ourselves available and inviting to those in pain. For us, the expression "shoulder to cry on" isn't a cliché; it's our way of life.

CHAPTER 6

SATURDAY, MARCH 14

*S*cott, is that you?"

Scott Gerard looks up quickly, but then stares at the shiny hospital floors. He doesn't know how good all my six senses are; he doesn't want me to see that he's been crying.

I walk toward him. He's got his hands stuffed in his pockets and his gray hoodie pulled over his head like he's trying to disappear. As always, much of Scott's face is partially hidden.

"Nice to see you again," he says, but his tone contradicts his words. No one is ever happy to see anyone at a hospital. Almost every gathering here relates to worry, sorrow, or goodbyes.

"Same here, Scott." Ever since talking with him in the library, I can't stop myself from thinking about him in *that* way. If Scott pulls toward me, I can more easily push Cody away.

"Why are you here?" he asks, still staring at the mirrorlike freshly mopped floor.

"I volunteer," I say, then pause, allowing him to ask for details, but he's silent. The hall echoes with the sounds of beeping equipment, weeping families, and footsteps of rushing nurses.

"So, Scott, is everything okay?" I ask, knowing the answer to that question is always no here in the ICU. I was running an errand for a nurse, since volunteers don't work here. I guess they don't want the young, hopeful people to see the awful agony of a person's final days.

"My grandmother," he mumbles, then points toward the room behind us.

"I'm sorry," I say. I've perfected this expression like a sympathy professional. He nods, and then I peek into the room to see a common scene: a human who is now more a machine than a person. Another ICU cyborg. "What's wrong with her?"

"Another stroke," he mumbles. Not a stroke, but another one. No wonder he's thinking about God; he's counting on a miracle. That's why he was so distracted the other day.

I take a step toward him, then ask softly, "How bad?"

"The doctors don't know yet," he says, then finally looks up. Not at me, at his grandmother's room. His hands come out of his pockets; they're balled into fists. In every lounge, I think the hospital should install a punching bag to release all the pent-up rage.

"I'm sorry, Scott," I say, and instinctively reach out a helping hand toward him.

"Thanks," he says, but in that one word and the look in his two eyes, I learn so much. His green eyes are fields of emotions, with rows of fear, anger, worry, and grief swaying together.

"If you need to talk to someone . . . ," I offer, almost a whisper.

"Thanks, Cassandra," he says. I flutter like a leaf on a tree when he speaks my name.

"There are people at the hospital, and then at school, you know—"

"The peer counseling thing," he says, interrupting and surprising me. He's never been in as far as I know. "That's a great idea."

"Really?" I say.

"I think it's great you try to help people," he says, taking a step back toward me. He sighs, then points into his grandmother's room. "She was—I mean is—like that."

"I'm here if you need me," I say very softly.

"That what she used to say," Scott says, his sighing sad face now cracking if not a smile, then something close to it. "My grandmother's a saint. I guess soon she'll be in heaven."

I let that go; instead, I inch closer. "What kind of person is she?"

Scott starts telling me stories about his grandmother. He talks about how he never knew his father, and his mom always worked two, sometimes three, jobs to support him and send him to Catholic school. They moved in with his grandmother, who raised him while his mom worked. After the last story, he musters a half smile, then says, "I've got to keep it together."

"What do you mean?"

"Like the other day in class. I think Mr. Abraham was getting angry with me for choosing faith over science. I can't afford anything other than an excellent grade in Honors Biology."

"Mr. A is all right," I assure Scott. "He's a tough teacher, but fair."

"I know, but I'm worried. It's going to be hard to get into a good college with the rep of Flint-area public schools. I wanted to stay at Powers. There just wasn't enough money."

"That's a good school."

"I want to go to med school and be a doctor," he says with pride in his voice at what he plans to do with his life. For some people, the future is all that pulls them through the present. Part of me wants to say, "I want to be a doctor too," but instead, I'll let Scott feel special.

"You should volunteer here," I tell him. "You'd learn a lot."

"I'd like to, but I don't have time to volunteer," he says. "I've got a job waiting tables."

"That's cool."

"Besides, I've already spent too much time in hospitals these last few years."

"What do you mean?" I ask, moving ever closer.

"Her husband, my grandfather," he says, looking back into the room. "Brain cancer. I watched him fall apart day by day. And that's when I knew I wanted to be a doctor. I know doctors can't cure everyone, but I want to help other families not go through the pain we went through."

"So, is he . . . ," I say, but trail off to let Scott fill in the blank about the void in his life.

"Six years ago," he says, then actually lets out a small laugh. An escape valve for emotional steam building up inside him. "It was the best of times, it was the worst of times."

"*A Tale of Two Cities*," I say, never shy about showing off my intelligence to smart guys.

"So, she's well read *too*," he says, making me wonder exactly what he means by "too."

I smile back. Like London and Paris, it seems we have many connections. Until now, he'd always seemed too shy, too secure, too centered. I like the vain but thin-skinned boys.

"When he was like this, in the ICU, I was so conflicted because—," Scott says, then stops.

"It's okay, Scott, you can trust me," I remind him. He lets out a loud sigh of relief.

"Before I'd walk into the room, I would pray to God that he was alive," he continues. "And then when I'd leave and think about his suffering, I'd pray that he'd be dead by morning."

"That's so sad."

"No human being should suffer like that," he says.

"The doctors do their best to ease people's pain."

"Drugs only help the patient, not the pain of the families," he says. "My grandmother hated to come see him in that condition. It was just so hard for her."

"It can be difficult to watch—"

"No, it was too hard for her not to want to reach over and pull the plugs from the machines keeping him alive. She used to come home after every visit and go on and on how she never wanted to end up like that. But now look at her," he says, on the edge of losing it.

Scott looks at his grandmother. He's talking about the past because she has no future.

"It's against the law. Even if it wasn't, the Church doesn't believe in euthanasia. Only God decides who lives and dies," he says, then turns back and our eyes meet in that special way. I've learned to listen not to what people say but how they say it. I watch them closely as they speak, in particular their eyes. Lips may lie, but the eyes never do. I know he doesn't believe what he says. He loves his grandmother and he wants her out of her misery. He believes in God and he believes in mercy; he's got to learn you can't believe in both and make it in this world.

"Scott, if there's anything I can do," I say.

"Thanks. I didn't know this about you."

"What do you mean?"

"I didn't know you worked here. I didn't know how much

you cared about people. I guess I didn't know you at all," he says, then smiles. "I guess that was my mistake."

I stay silent so he'll keep talking. "We both know why," he says.

I shake my head, then ask, "What do you mean?"

"You on Facebook or MySpace?" is his strange follow-up. I nod my head. I'm not into it like so many people at school, but like earrings, these sites are a required Lapeer High female accessory. I'm one of the few who have both. Facebook connects me to people at the center, like Robyn, while MySpace allows me access to Samantha and others who dwell on the fringes.

"From what I hear, every girl writes how they want a guy who is funny, kind, and smart," Scott says. He's not looking at me anymore; rather, he's not letting me look at him.

"So?"

"Well, I'm funny, kind, and smart, so why have I only had one girlfriend in high school?" he asks. "And that girl, well, Samantha has a lot of problems, including her judgment in men." Again, there's no eye contact, which is good for me. He'd see my eyes lighting up like somebody hitting the jackpot. Cute guys like Cody act confident because life is easy for them, so when things get hard or go wrong, they're totally crushed. They're so hot, they easily melt and grow soft. Scott's right; he's not a hottie. I've learned, however, that it is the look in a boy's eye, not his looks, that matters most. Scott's green eyes reveal a field of hurt needing healing.

"Well, this year isn't over yet," I respond in the best flirting voice I can summon. I pause for a second, as I pull out one of the hospital pads I use to take notes. I write down my cell phone number, then offer it to him. His hand shakes a little as he reaches out.

"If you need to call," I say as he takes the paper from my hand. I let my hand linger.

"I'll do that," he says. "But what about Cody?"

"It's just a phone number, not a marriage proposal," I say, then laugh.

"I don't want any problem with Cody," he says. "I have enough problems."

"Don't worry about him," I say. "He's nothing to fear."

"Unlike you, from what I hear," he says, almost in a whisper.

"I don't know what you've heard," I counter.

"I heard you're a heartbreaker," he says.

"Sounds like your heart is already broken," I purr. "So . . ."

He manages a laugh, then says, "So maybe I got nothing to lose."

"Maybe so, Scott."

"Well, almost nothing," he says as the dark cloud returns to his face. "I have to go."

"I understand," I say. I turn around toward the elevator. Just before I enter, I look back at Scott. He's standing at the door of his grandmother's room—probably her deathbed—like there's something in his way. I sense, even from this distance, that he's taking deep breaths, which slowly turn into the familiar hospital soundtrack of sniffles, sobbing, and stifled screams.

The rest of my shift is uneventful. I check in with Scott a few times, and he seems happy to see me each time. I think about asking him for a ride home in his car (he calls his Chevy Cobalt the "no volt") but it seems too much to ask too soon. Instead, Maggie picks me up at work. I don't pick a fight, and she manages not to mention Alexei the entire ride. With the reunion coming up, everyone is trying to get along. Veronica wouldn't have it any other way.

Since I arrive on time and without incident, Mom has nothing to say to me. Unless there's conflict, we barely communicate. I pass by the living room. She sits listening to classical music and sipping a bottle of water. Maggie heads into the kitchen, while Veronica remains in her room. I'll need to see her sometime tonight; she always wants to see me after I volunteer at the hospital. She usually lights up after I visit; it's as if she's the bulb and I'm her battery.

Once I get into my room, I think about calling Scott, but it seems too soon for even that. I need to deal with Cody; I need to comfort Robyn; I need to focus on my family.

I call Robyn, but she's still not answering her phone. I don't want to call her home phone, just in case one of her parents picks up again. I can't be the one to tell them. It's one thing to stir up the bubbling pot of high school drama, but this is beyond that. I look for her online, but she's not there either. I seek out Scott online, but he's off the grid, it would seem. I pull up Samantha Dressen's MySpace page. She's online, but her profile remains set to private. I see that her profile name has changed to "I Hurt, Hurt, Hurt" and that her new profile picture is a work of art: a black-and-white photo of her with the colors inverted. Very artsy, very strange, very Samantha. From what I've observed, Samantha's one of these girls with six hundred friends online and none in real life. I send another friend request in the virtual world, and vow to make one more real-world attempt. She'll probably reject me; I'm sure rejection is one of her gifts.

Before I log off, I find another news story, then print and file it. One of the hardest things for Robyn in dealing with Craig breaking up with her is that it took her by surprise. What Robyn doesn't realize is that out of the blue is the best way for awful events to occur. Better to have the lights turned out all at once than to slowly succumb to a looming darkness.

NEWS REPORT #3

Another child has disappeared in the mid-Michigan area. Twelve-year-old Jason Hamilton was last seen at Midland Middle School on Friday, March 13. According to his friends, Hamilton left the park after an altercation during a basketball game that left him both crying and bleeding. Police believe this disappearance might be connected to a similar incident that occurred about a week ago in the Bay City area. In that case, an eleven-year-old was reported missing but appeared days later back near the playground where he had been abducted. The police report that the Bay City boy was pulled into a black Ford van, blindfolded, and gagged. Police are not releasing any other details or officially discussing any possible motives. One anonymous police source described the entire incident as "odd" because the only thing the perpetrator achieved was terrifying the child. The source added, "It seemed like all the perp wanted to do was make the kid cry."

CHAPTER 7

MONDAY, MARCH 16

I'm sorry, Cody. You know that, right?"

"I don't believe you!" he shouts.

We're in his basement, surrounded by his sports memorabilia, electronic toys, and sweaty memories. Cody—like Tyler and my other boyfriends before him—is not welcome at my house. And since I never allow breakups to occur in public or in parked cars, we're sharing this private space one last time. Tonight, both of us are standing, although Cody looks ready to crumble.

"Cody, it just isn't working out," I say, softly. "I adore you. I want you to be happy."

"I *am* happy," he says. "And you don't know what I want. I want you, Cass."

I try to reach out to him, but he turns away. He readjusts his backward-turned Detroit Tigers ball cap, then stomps to the other side of the room. He sits on the sofa—the place where I gave him most of what he wanted—and pouts like some two-year-old.

"Cody, baby, I'm sorry." I'm standing still, unsure which way the wind is blowing.

"I want my jacket!" he shouts. I unsnap it and throw it to him. It feels like a weight has lifted.

"Cody, it's okay to be upset," I reassure him in a tone I've used a lot in our six months together. Last fall, when the school's football team lost in the playoffs, we left the end-of-season party early. After a few beers, Cody poured out his disappointment, crying on my shoulder rather than in his beer. Now he's suffered another setback, and I need to help him.

He puts the jacket on, then says, "All my friends told me you played games."

"I don't want to play games. I just need to end this," I say.

"More games," he says. "Like all the other times."

"No, this is it," I say, trying to remember if our six other breakup scenes contained my announcement of the finality. "We're through."

"Is it Craig?" he says. "How could you do that to your best friend?"

"It's not Craig," I say. "I wouldn't do anything to hurt Robyn."

"I bet it's that freak Scott Gerard. Kelsey said she saw the two of you in the library just laughing it up," he says. Anyone who is not an athlete is a freak in Cody's eyes.

"Who are you to talk!" I shout, ensuring the tension continues to build. "I know all about you and Burnt Knees! She's doing both you and Craig. Teammates in everything."

"That's a lie," he counters.

"That's not what I heard," I say, which is a lie.

"I'm not cheating on you," he counters. "You are the one who is—"

"Why do you think there's someone else?" I ask, then start my breakup speech. I've said it so many times it bores me. I start with, "It's not you, Cody. You're so sweet and sexy."

He responds as expected; a thin smile wipes out his angry glare. I motion for him to sit with me on the sofa. As he sits next to me, I take his hands in mine.

"But I know it's just not working. Prom is coming up," I say. There's always some marker coming up in high school. This is the fill-in-the-blank part of the speech. "And you should be with someone who can make you happy. That's not me, babe, that's not me."

"I need you," is his answer. He's toughing it out, so I'll take another tack to get his tears.

"Okay, Cody, baby, it's not you and it's not me," I say as softly as I can. "It's my family, my mom in particular."

"I know she doesn't like me," he says.

"That's not it," I continue. "She doesn't want me dating in high school and getting involved. She has plans for me, and whenever she sees I'm getting serious about someone . . ."

"Serious?" he says, his trademark smirk almost returning to his face.

"I love you, Cody," I say, using a smile to camouflage my lie. "That's why we can't see each other anymore. You'll just get hurt more. This is for the best. You understand?"

He's silent, taking it all in. I move closer, then kiss him on the cheek. "It's over, Cody, for good. I understand if you're angry and upset. I know we can stay friends."

He stares back at me in horror as if I were a monster. "What are you talking about?"

"You'll see over time this was right, and you'll want us to be friends," I tell him, still gently stroking the side of his face. "You'll need a shoulder to cry on, and I'll be there for you."

He stares deeper now, eyes like drills. "You bitch."

"What?"

"You bitch," he repeats, almost leaping off the sofa. "You want me hurt."

"Cody, you're talking crazy. You don't—"

"Do you remember how we started going out?" he asks, but I don't want to answer. "I was at Saint Dominic's Church. You were an altar server at my uncle's funeral. I was sitting in the front pew. I was crying because I knew my mom was upset. You winked at me."

"That's not true," I half lie. I didn't wink, but I did make contact with his damp eyes.

"At school the next week, you came on to me," he says.

"None of us could figure it out. You'd never talked to me before. Then, bam, you're giving it up before breaking up with Tyler."

I just look at the floor as Cody stares into our past. He's right so far about how wrong I treated him. Finally, I mutter, "At first, I thought you were just another jock like Tyler, but I learned you were better than him. I thought it would work out, but it can't. I'm sorry."

"So am I," he says, adding, "I'm sorry I ever met you."

"Cody, baby, please—"

He stomps past me toward the far side of the furnished basement. On the paneled wall hang some of his sports awards and certificates, mostly for participation. Cody's not a star. He's the second-string cog that keeps sports teams churning along. He's in it for the letters and the ladies.

"I hate you," he shouts.

"You hate me because you loved me," I say as I follow him to the other side of the room.

"I don't care what you say or think!" he shouts back, shaking a fist at me. "Maybe that's why Scott likes you, because you're just like Samantha Dracula."

"What do you mean?" I ask about his sudden insight.

"You're a monster!" he shouts.

"Cody, there are no such things as monsters," I say, laughing it off, but he's staring through me. He takes a step toward me, and I recoil. He quickly turns and slams his fist into the paneled wall.

"I hate you!" he shouts while slamming his fist repeatedly. Upstairs I hear chairs moving. Time is running out for me to get what I need from Cody one last time.

"Let it out," I say, then slowly approach him. His fist slams against the wall again. The force knocks one of the glass-framed certificates to the floor. Blood spurts from his hand.

"Stay away from me," he says, waving his bloody hand in my face.

He stares at me as he moves his bloody hand against his long white wannabe gangsta T-shirt. A crimson pool forms over his heart and I whisper, "I'm sorry, Cody." He takes a deep breath, sighs, and the anger leaves him, washed away by tears forming at the corners of his eyes.

"It's okay to cry, Cody," I whisper, and he takes a step toward me. I try to avoid the blood pooling on his shirt, and instead let his head fall onto my shoulder. I take the tie-dyed bandanna from my head and wrap his hand to stop the bleeding. The door opens upstairs, and Cody's parents come to his rescue. Before they arrive, I take the monogrammed handkerchief from my pocket and wipe away his tears. There are only a few, but like an expensive perfume or a narcotic drug, it takes just a tiny amount to make a big difference. I'm flush as I walk upstairs.

Cody's mom drives me home. She's just staring at the road while I'm listening to *Abbey Road* on my iPod. We've never had anything to talk about before; now we don't even fake it.

It is the same world of silence when I return home. Everybody's doors are closed. I sneak into Veronica's room to deposit the monogrammed handkerchief sprinkled with Cody's tears on the table next to the bed. She could thank me in the morning, but she never does. There's no gratitude for duty; there's never a celebration of my sacrifices.

I jump online, quickly checking news alerts to add to my folder, but there's nothing, yet. I glance at Cody's page, but he's yet to change his Facebook status to show that he's single. Robyn's not online either; she hasn't been for over a week. Just like she hasn't returned to school. I call her cell, but she doesn't pick up. I leave another message, invite myself over to dinner with her family tomorrow, and set my phone by the computer.

Robyn's Facebook page remains intact from ten days ago. It's as if she's fallen into a coma. Maybe she's being sentimental or maybe it's wishful thinking, like the whole thing's a bad dream and she'll wake up with Craig back in her life. I click on Brittney's busy page that contains over a thousand photos, mostly of herself. I wonder if she fears Alzheimer's and that's why she photographs seemingly every day of her life. It's clear from the page that Robyn was never Brittney's best friend; Brittney's best friend is her camera. All the photos look the same: overexposed cleavage and emptied vodka bottles. There are gang signs, stoned group shots, and multiple attempts for weak white girls with wealthy parents to act ghetto. It's all so silly but also a little sad, and yet I totally understand wanting to be something you're not.

With Cody out of the picture, I'll need to quickly find some new emotional resources. I look for Scott again online, but find nothing. I search out Samantha. As always, she's online. She ignored my latest friend request, but I'm persistent and patient, so I send another. On this one, I also send the message, "Hey, Samantha. Time for a truce. I don't want to be enemies, so all that leaves is becoming friends." I want to get inside her page; I need to get inside her head.

I search the news for updates, then do a last check of Cody's page. What I find confirms he knows this breakup is final. Sometime in the past hour, he's erased our six months together.

Just as I'm about to call it a night, my phone rings. The ringtone of "Imagine" lets me know Robyn is alive and well. I tell her about my breakup with Cody, although not in detail. She continues to talk about her breakup with Craig in detail, but for someone as smart as Robyn, I'm surprised that she doesn't see the big picture. Yes, she's heartbroken over the loss of love coupled with the sense of betrayal, but I sense it is more than that. People like Robyn, who are used to success, often are not resilient and overreact when things go wrong. Robyn's perfect world has crashed around her. She now questions everything, even her self-worth as a person. She can't see (and I can't tell her) that she can survive without a boyfriend; it just takes time. We talk deep into the morning, but I feel my energy level drain toward empty. Like most of our time together, Cody took more energy than he gave, even in our breakup.

I say good-bye, then Robyn says, "It's okay, Cass, there's nothing left to say."

"I'll see you at school tomorrow, right?" I ask.

"Tomorrow morning for sure, I promise," she says. I don't remind her she said the same thing about showing up this morning.

"Maybe after school, I'll come over for dinner. What do you think?"

"I'd like that," she says, then adds, "and Becca would love it."

"It's a deal."

There's a short pause, then Robyn says, "Thanks for everything, Cass."

"I'm here—or there—whenever you need a shoulder to cry on," I remind her.

She laughs; a laugh not of amusement, but one of total exhaustion. "I don't think I have any more tears left to cry."

"There's always more tears," I say with total confidence. "They are infinite."

It's like the phone goes dead with sixty seconds of total silence. "Robyn, are you there?"

There's still more silence, then Robyn says, "Tomorrow morning, I'm getting up, looking in the mirror, putting on my smile again, and all of this hurting is going to stop."

I try to imagine her on the other end of the phone. "I'll see you tomorrow then?" I ask.

But once again it is as if the phone's dead; there's no answer, like I'm talking into a void.

"Robyn, this isn't funny," I say.

Still no answer.

"Robyn, please, are you there?"

"I was just practicing my smile," she finally says.

"Give it time. You won't need to practice or fake it, it will come back," I say.

"Along with those infinite tears," she says after another long, scary pause.

"I gotta go," I whisper. "I'll see you tomorrow. You promised, remember."

"Cass, just one more thing, okay?" Robyn asks.

"What's that?"

She pauses, then says, "Thanks for everything. I love you, Cassandra. Good-bye."

CHAPTER 8

WEDNESDAY, MARCH 18

What's going on?"

Like a fire alarm, there's loud ringing everywhere. It sounds like every phone in every purse and pocket is ringing simultaneously. I'm in sixth-period history class, the only class I share with Brittney and Robyn. Given the history between us, somehow that seems right. Robyn, however, isn't in school. I'd call her, but Mr. A snatched my phone this morning.

"What's wrong?" I say to Brittney. She turns to look at me; her heavily made-up face starts to drain. All around the room, I see similar looks, especially among the most popular girls.

"It's Robyn," she says.

"What about her?"

Brittney's wearing a shocked smile on her face as she answers, "She's dead."

Our history teacher, Mr. Lane, looks befuddled as most of the class ignores the tragedies of the past to deal with the one before us. I bolt from my chair and race out the door. During first period, Mr. Abraham caught me answering my phone. It was Robyn. Before I could shut off the phone or speak to her, he took my cell per school rules. Those rules don't apply now.

I race down the halls like the anchor in a relay. I burst into the door of Mr. A's room, and his blue eyes grow wide. The room is full of freshmen; they don't have a clue.

"Cassandra, what are you doing here?" he asks, more annoyed than angry.

"I need my phone!" I shout.

"I'm sorry, but the—"

"Something's happened with Robyn," I say, and I hear a murmur go through the class. There are lots of girls at school named Robyn, but just the way I say it, everybody knows who I mean. I pause, then speak loud enough for everyone to hear as I say, "Robyn's dead."

He ignores the gasps, then reaches into his desk to hand me my phone. I turn it on, and there are six messages. One's from Robyn's cell, which was from first period, and then two from her home number two hours later. I don't recognize the last three calls, one just ten minutes ago.

I pick up the last message first. It's Robyn's dad. His voice crackles like sparks. A car crash. Holly Rec Area. The EMTs tried. Massive brain damage. At the hospital now. I rush out into the hall, then push Return Call. Mr. Berry picks up. Before he speaks, I say, "I'm so sorry."

He doesn't speak; the language of death is new to him.

I wait, then finally ask, "Where's Becca?"

There's no reply as my words echo off towers and satellites, so I ask, "What can I do?"

"There's nothing to do," he said, defeated. His words are nails driving into his heart.

"Is Becca there with you?"

"No, we didn't want to upset her," he says. "My sister is meeting her at home."

"I'm leaving school so I'm there when she gets home," I say. "Unless you need me at the hospital. Just tell me what you want me to do."

There's quiet. He's overwhelmed by events; he can't choose. He probably can barely manage to pull air into his lungs and push it back out. He's acting only on animal instinct.

I think of calling Mom, but decide against it. Instead, I look in the parking lot for Scott's Cobalt, easy to spot with the Powers bumper sticker. Inside, I see a backseat filled with books, CDs, and clothes. When the final bell rings, everyone leaving school appears to be moving in slow motion. Even from the distance, I sense the moist tears in everyone's eyes.

"Did you hear?" Scott shouts once he spots me leaning against his car.

"I heard," I reply softly, then look at the ground, hiding my eyes from him. "I need a ride."

"You don't drive?" he asks, and I shake my head.

"I need to get to Robyn's house," I say. Scott opens the door for me, and I climb in.

"Okay, sure, just tell me where to go," he says. He climbs in and quickly pulls out of the parking lot. The juniors gathered by the front doors all have the same dazed look, like people who've just witnessed an accident. I want to be with them, but I need to be next to Becca.

I give Scott directions, and then I lapse into silence, staring out the window. Life's not real now; it's another movie that I'm looking at on a screen. Scott tries to talk, but I shut him down, nicely. I can't talk; it is taking all of my energy to hide my dark, swelling human emotions.

"Thanks, Scott, thanks for everything. I owe you," I say when he drops me off. I kiss him on the cheek. He smiles in surprise and delight. That's nice, that's enough, for now. For now.

Robyn's aunt greets me. Like her brother, this woman can barely speak.

"I'm so sorry," I say. "How much misfortune can one family withstand?"

My question prompts not an answer, but a gusher of grief. I comfort her, the best I can. Like people I meet at the hospital, she's a stranger made instantly intimate through tragedy. I let her cry long and hard. Without Cody's jacket, my bare shoulders easily swallow her sorrow.

"Becca's upstairs," she says through sniffles.

"Does she know yet?" I ask.

"I just told her Robyn had to do something after school with her parents," she says, still sounding distraught. "I've made it worse."

"You had to lie," I say. "What is happening now?"

"I heard from my brother. They've got decisions to make. Then they'll be coming home," she says. Her tone is one of shock. People never expect the inevitable demon of death to touch them. "I need to go and be with my brother at the hospital."

"I'll stay with Becca," I say. She doesn't answer. Instead, she gives me another hug as she heads out the door. I'm not related, but in the shadow of death, people pull together like one large family. Tragedy creates human connections, even as it severs the mortal coil.

I go upstairs. Before I check in on Becca, I look around Robyn's room. I'm wondering what secrets she's hidden from her family and me. I look through desk and dresser drawers, but I find nothing but evidence of Robyn's desire for perfection: makeup, study guides, and a mirror on every table. I log on to her computer, then her Facebook page using her password, "Becca4ever." I hunt around for a while, but there's nothing—nothing to tell me that this crash wasn't an accident. I take a moment to check my messages and they're overflowing. Death creates a flood of words. This is Lapeer's Hurricane Katrina and September 11th. I check a news alert, see the story, make a quick printout, and then shut down Robyn's computer.

I get ready to close the door when it hits me: I'll probably never walk in this room again. I soak up all the good times, but mostly the tears, and head for the door. I stop, however, when I see the smoking gun. On a small table, by her door, buried under makeup jars is Robyn's iPod. Did she know she wouldn't need it again? Did she know she was taking her last ride?

I peek into Becca's room. She's playing a fantasy video game. This is just another day for her; another of her last days. She doesn't know that, in the time it takes to click that mouse in her fantasy world, her parents, and everyone who knew Robyn, now live in a real world changed forever. In Becca, death lingers; in Robyn, death took seconds and it had mercy.

"What are you doing here, Cass?" she asks, staring at me rather than the screen.

"I thought I'd come visit," I say, forcing a smile.

"Great!" she shouts.

"Great!" I shout louder, even if the stronger part of me wants to whisper the tragic news.

"Who keeps calling?" she asks. The phones in the house have been ringing nonstop almost since I arrived, but I won't pick up. Becca wants to, but her parents forbid her to answer the phone. More protection; more water in the moat they've tried to build around her.

"I bet it's *American Idol* calling to invite you on," I say.

Robyn told me that her parents approached the Make-a-Wish Foundation, but have not heard back. We talk for a while, mostly about nothing at all. I try not to say much, since it would only create more lies I'll have to remember, more trust that I'm already stretching to the heartbreaking point. She needs to trust me. We then play a video game, which I let her win. It only seems right.

Just as we're about to play another game, I hear the garage door. I take a big sip from my water bottle and head downstairs toward the opening front door. Mr. Berry is holding up his wife like she's been shot in the legs and can't walk on her own. He looks like he's been shot in the heart and head. "I'm so sorry," I say almost the second they walk in the front door.

"Our sweet baby girl is gone." Mr. Berry mutters these six short words, barely discernable over his wife's countless sobs. They turn to look at each other seeking strength, but it doesn't come.

"I need to sit down," Mrs. Berry says, then stumbles to the sofa. She collapses into the soft fabric as the hard truth of Robyn's death hits. Robyn will never walk in the door again, and every time her parents walk in the door, they'll remember that cruel fact. It won't be the big things, but the small things that will come later, last longer, and cling to them like a thirsty leech.

I sit next to Mrs. Berry on the sofa. I offer her my handkerchief, but she refuses.

"Please, it is the least I can do," I say, almost begging. "Let me do something."

"You are, were, are a good friend to Robyn." Her tenses tangled; her voice strangled.

"What happened?" I ask Mr. Berry.

"I told her not to drive so fast," is all Mr. Berry says. I know there are so many things I can say, but now is not the time. They're at their grief limit; they have very little more to give.

"It's not your fault, John," Mrs. Berry whispers. Her voice is parched; she's cried out. Like a sponge expelled from the sea and left out in the sun, she's dehydrated and nearly dead. While there seems to be a limit on grief, the threshold on guilt is much higher.

"What about Becca?" I ask Mr. Berry.

"We'll have to tell her," he says, but he's not talking to me. He's answering on autopilot.

"Do you want me to do it?" I ask.

"That's sweet of you," Mrs. Berry says. "But that's a parent's responsibility."

"I just want to do whatever I can to make this easier on all of you," I say. "Robyn was like a sister, and Becca means so much to me."

"Thank you, but we'll need to do it," Mr. Berry says. "I just don't know how. How do you tell a dying child that the person she loves the most won't be there anymore?"

"I want to be strong for Becca," I say instead of answering the question. "That's what Robyn would have wanted."

"Would have wanted," Mr. Berry repeats and the past tense knocks the wind out of him. He buckles onto the sofa now, next to his wife. I hand him my handkerchief, but he's fighting it. He's a good man, but he's a *man*. He doesn't want to cry; he wants to be strong. For him, there's no strength in tears.

"I'll take care of things at school, if that's okay with you," I say, but that statement only leads to bewildered looks from both. Maybe my question forces Robyn's parents' realization of the hundreds of details to attend to, the thousands of conversations to have, and the millions of tears they'll cry. Now they can't find even one word—yes or no—to say. Before a tragedy, people think they know everything; afterward, they realize that so much of reality is just an illusion.

"I'll talk to Mr. Abraham; we'll organize something," I add as they remain mute. "Everybody loved Robyn. They'll need some way to show it."

"Thank you, thank you for everything. You're so giving," Mr. Berry says as he hands me back my handkerchief that, at the last moment, he moistened with a few of his tough-man tears.

"I just want to do what's best for everyone," I say, thinking not just about this family in front of me, but also back at Veronica's house. I go upstairs and say good-bye to Becca. I can't look her in the eye because I know the storm that is coming. Part of me wants to stay for the suffering; I wonder if that part of me died with Robyn.

When I get home, everyone is sitting at the table. I want to run past them, but I can't; they are my family. Instead, I pull the grief-stained handkerchief from my pocket and offer it to

Veronica, who is feeling better, mostly thanks to me, and spending more time downstairs. Veronica takes it without a word or even a nod. I turn on my heel and head toward my room. But I get no farther than one step away when Mom calls after me. "What's going on?"

Although we keep our secrets safe from the world, inside this house it is hard to hide anything from my family's sixth sense. I look down, then mutter, "My best friend, Robyn, died. I think she killed herself." I don't add that even if I'm not to blame, I'm partly responsible.

As I walk away, I try to pretend I didn't hear Veronica proclaim, "That's just wonderful."

CHAPTER 9

THURSDAY, MARCH 19

Why were you surprised?"

I direct the question back at Scott. I'm sitting in my bedroom in the twilight with the lights off, thinking about Veronica saying Robyn's death was "just wonderful." With just two words, everything I've known suddenly seems wrong. I was lost in brooding thoughts about family and friends, about betrayal and loyalty, when Scott called. After a first few awkward moments, we're connecting. The talk turns to Robyn; it is all anyone at school is talking about.

"I was just surprised you came to school, that's all I was saying," Scott says in the tone of an apology. "Lots of Robyn's friends, I noticed, didn't come to school today."

"I wanted to be there for people, I guess," I say, telling more truth than he can imagine. The school was filled with waves of tears, and I rode every one. I spent most of the day not in class, but in public areas, like the library, providing comfort. By the end of the day, every friend of Robyn's who came to school came to me. Many cried endlessly; I took their tears effortlessly.

"I should have been there for you," he says.

"What do you mean?"

"Yesterday, in the car, I wasn't much help."

"Yes you were, Scott, you helped a lot."

"Really?"

"Sometimes the best thing to do is nothing," I say, knowing those words reflect badly back at me. I think of all the things I said—and didn't say—to Robyn. I betrayed Robyn; I obeyed my family. I had no choice. There may be another Robyn, but I'll never have another family. Yet, after Veronica's words last night, I wonder if that reality might not be so bad after all.

"Well, if you do want to talk," Scott says, "I'm a good listener."

I laugh. Mostly guys only want to listen when you tell them how great they are. That was Cody; that was Tyler. I sense that's not Scott. "Thanks, Scott, but that's my job."

"What do you mean?" he asks. I don't respond right away, and he allows the silence.

I've said too much, but something about Scott pulls the truth—or as much truth as I can speak—out of me. Finally, I say, "I'm the one who listens to other people's problems."

"Then who listens to *your* problems?" Before I can answer, he laughs nervously and adds, "Never mind. I bet a beautiful, smart girl like you doesn't have any problems."

Silence surrounds me. I wish I could tell Scott my truth—a

truth I've always known but that the events of the past few days have opened like a flower. I don't have any problems; I *am* the problem. Scott lets the silence linger, which most guys won't do, and then says, "I'm sorry."

"Sorry?"

"I'm as smooth at this as broken glass," he says.

"At what?"

"I'm trying to flirt with you," he whispers. "I guess if I have to tell you that, then—"

I cut him off, yet pull him closer. "It's not flirting if the person already likes you."

"Really?"

"Really," I say, and then the silence swallows again.

"So, do you want to go out sometime?" he asks, but before I can answer he adds, "Sorry, that's rude. Your best friend just died and I'm asking you out. What must you think of me?"

"What I think of you," I say without a pause, "is that I'll see you Saturday night."

After I hang up, I head downstairs to get a fresh bottle of water. In the past hour, I've heard both Maggie and Mom come home from working their usual ten-hour days. Earlier today, Veronica left the house for the first time in a while, but now she's back in her room, waiting for me. This morning she didn't say good-bye to me, and this evening, she won't say thank you. So her last words that still echo are how she told me Robyn's death was "just wonderful."

Mom's on the phone, no doubt handling last-minute arrangements for the family reunion. Maggie, sitting at the kitchen table, motions for me to join her. I stop but don't sit down.

"How was school?" Maggie asks. "You could probably swim through the tears."

"Most of Robyn's other friends didn't come to school today," I report. "But tomorrow we're doing a memorial service, so most of them will probably be there."

Maggie smiles and says, "Veronica's very pleased with you."

"She shouldn't be," I say sharply. "It wasn't my fault."

"I know that," Maggie says. "You're a good girl, Cassandra, you follow the rules."

I look away from her. As with doctors, the family rule is "Do no harm." No harm directly. But it is through hurt that my family thrives. Since Maggie opened this door, I step in. "Unlike Alexei."

"What do you mean?"

"There's something evil about him. I just know it," I say, finally telling her about my suspicions. Maybe I'll go up to my room, unlock the desk drawer, and bring her the folder full of evidence.

"How dare you talk that way about your *promised* cousin," she says.

"Don't remind me." Both Alexei and I turned seventeen this year. My family says they have plans for me, but they haven't given me any specifics. I only know that it involves Alexei. So I'm pretty sure that whatever it is, it will be bad for me.

"You don't have to like him," she says. Love, of course, isn't in our family lexicon.

"I *loathe* him," I whisper.

"Cassandra Veronica Gray! He is family. How dare you talk that way?"

I pause, think of all the things I want to say, and then say them: "I hate him and this life we lead. I don't want a family that's happy when my friends die. I just want to be normal and—"

But she stops me with a hard stare and a hard slap of her hand against the kitchen table. "Cassandra, none of us chose this existence. No more than a worm chooses to be worm, a lion chooses to be a lion, or a human chooses to be a human. This is who you are!"

"No, it is not who I am!" I shout back. "It is *what* I am."

"We are family!" she shouts. "We all have our roles. You have yours. I have mine."

"And what is that?"

"Your role now is to produce the next generation," is her horrifying reply.

"And what if I don't want to?"

"You don't have a choice," she says in a tone that sucks all the moisture out of the air.

"Then explain Siobhan," I say, hissing the forbidden name of the family exile.

"I don't know anyone by that name," she says as she rises from the table. She walks toward me and points her finger at me. "I don't know anyone by that name, and *neither do you.*"

Maggie starts to walk past me, but I take off running in a different direction. I'm sitting on a curb at the end of the block dialing my phone before she's probably climbed the first stair.

"Siobhan, it's your cousin Cassandra." The phone shakes in my hand as I speak into it.

"You're not supposed to call me," is her less-than-friendly greeting.

"I know, but I don't have anywhere else to turn."

"What about Lillith or Mara?" she asks, naming my two other favorite cousins.

"They don't understand," I say. "They accept it."

She doesn't ask what "it" means. It is the life we lead. "No one knows you're calling?"

"I'm down the street," I say. "They don't know where I am. They don't care."

"You're wrong, Cassy; they care very much." I smile at hearing her nickname for me; it reminds us both of our connection. "I've hurt the family too much already. I can't talk to you."

"Can't? What do you mean?"

"I'm out of the family. It's all in the past," she says. "I can't get involved. It's wrong."

"But I have to tell you something, and it's important," I say. "Please, I've got no one else."

There's a long pause on the other end of the line until she finally says, "Okay, Cassy."

"My best friend, Robyn, died."

"What happened?"

I tell her a short version of Robyn's death, focusing on the rumors, not mentioning my hand in any of it. But my hands aren't clean; they still feel very damp with her blood.

"She killed herself?" Siobhan asks. I start to answer but instead I pause, letting a million thoughts in my head crash like waves on the beach. "Please don't tell me that you—"

I interrupt. "I wasn't in the car when she drove too fast. I didn't do anything directly."

"You're sure?" She seems skeptical.

"I did not," I say firmly. "But it was my fault. I know it was my fault."

"What did Veronica say?"

I pause, not wanting to repeat the words. "Let's just say it was beyond cruel."

"Get used to it," Siobhan says. "That is what your life is going to be like."

"I know," I say, wishing the stars above could swallow me. "Is that why you—?"

"Got out," she says. "That's part of it."

"Can you tell me how?" A five-word question that holds infinite possibilities for me.

"I can't tell you that, Cassy," she says. Regret drips in her voice.

"Why not?"

"Because part of it is figuring it out for yourself," she says. "I'm not the first. Others have left, but life becomes hard in a different way. I know you don't want to hear this, but your life is easy. The hardest thing in the world to do is love. You don't need to worry about that."

"But I want to!" I shout. "I want to fall in love. I want to be normal. I need to know!"

"Cassy, listen. I understand what you're going through," she says. "Everybody goes through this. Everybody pushes through it, and life goes on. Everybody fills their role—"

I cut her off. "But you got out."

"Yes, because I allowed myself to fall in love," she says. "But I'll always regret what I had to do to get out. And now that I am out, I'm an orphan. I have no family to protect me."

"But you have love," I say. "And you have a life that's not filled with tears."

"You're wrong about that," she says, almost laughing. "There's a difference."

"What's that?"

"The tears are all my own now."

"I don't understand," I say. "I thought love made you happy."

"And anything that makes you happy can make you sad,"

she says. "Cassy, look, I can't talk to you. I betrayed our family once; I can't do it again. I can't help you."

"Just tell me one thing!" I shout. "Please, just give me a hint, anything."

Another long pause. "Okay, but after this, you can't call me again. I'm out of this."

"I understand," I say. If you got out of jail, I suspect you'd never want to see iron bars again.

There's a pause, then she says, "Cassy, the hardest choice is the first choice."

"What do you mean?" I ask, even as the school bell rings across the street.

"The first choice," she finishes, "is realizing you have a choice."

CHAPTER 10

FRIDAY, MARCH 20

What do you want us to do?"

Brittney and I are both staring at Mr. Abraham. It has been about forty hours since Robyn's death, but it is only five short minutes before the memorial gathering at school. I'm waiting for an answer to my question about what to do, both right now and from this day forth.

"This isn't what she would have wanted," Brittney says in her best fit-throwing voice.

"It's too late to change everything," I tell her, but I'm focusing all my energy on Mr. Abraham. He, along with the peer counselors and school counselors, quickly organized this event. The theater auditorium is filling with traumatized students, but all the drama is backstage.

"You should have involved us," Brittney says. She's the spokesperson for Robyn's cheerleader friends. Like everyone else in school, their reaction to Robyn's death has been to walk around school like ants with a dead queen. "This should be upbeat, like Robyn was."

"This is a memorial service, not some kegger," I say, sharply and directly.

"We should be celebrating Robyn's life, that's what she would have wanted," she says.

"This isn't just about Robyn, this is about everybody left behind," I say. "What Robyn would have wanted and how she lived was to focus on other people. Her friends need to heal."

"That's sick," Brittney says.

"That's enough, both of you," Mr. A finally says, then sighs. He sips from his thermos, then says, "One thing's for sure, Robyn wouldn't want her friends fighting."

Both Brittney and I let that go. For now. Robyn was able to keep our rivalry in check, but if Brittney says one more word, then I'll bring up Craig and force her guilt down her throat.

"Brittney, I will help you plan something next week to be a celebration of Robyn's life," he says, as I try to hide a victor's smile. "But there's a process to grieving, and a memorial service like this—where people can openly grieve—is important to students healing and moving on. I wish we had more time to plan, but it's essential we do something before the weekend."

"I knew it," she hisses.

"I'm sorry, but we'll continue with the program that

Cassandra and the counselors have planned," he says. "I hope you will still say something as you agreed."

"I'd do anything for Robyn," Brittney says, trying to play the part of the martyr.

"Haven't you done enough?" I say. She stares daggers and I welcome the cuts.

"Brittney. This is difficult for everyone, especially her friends like you and Cassandra," Mr. Abraham says. He's one of the smartest people I know. Why can't he see through her?

"I *was* her best friend," Brittney says, treating this occasion like a fight on the playground. I've never felt the deep dark human emotion of hate, but it's emerging now.

"If that's the case, then—," I start, but I feel a hand on my shoulder. I turn around to see Dr. Albrecht, the school's main counselor.

"Cassandra, Brittney, please," she says. "I know this is hard for everyone."

"Then why isn't everyone here?" Brittney asks, sneaking a peek through the curtains. Dr. Albrecht decided to open the memorial service to anyone who knew Robyn and wanted to attend. I wanted it to be for everyone at school, but Dr. Albrecht said that wasn't the best way.

"Brittney, everybody in this school is changed by a student's death, I understand that," she continues. "But not everyone handles grief the same way. Some people grieve in private, some need to be around others. The thing we don't want to do is force students to behave one way or the other. You'll find all sorts of reactions from people."

"I understand," Brittney says, although I doubt she really does. When you spend half your life taking pictures of yourself, how can you even begin to understand other people?

I look through the curtains to see the room filled with students from across the spectrum, although it is mostly Robyn's fellow juniors.

"Brittney, there's no one right way to handle the death of a popular student," Dr. Albrecht says. "We're doing our best. We're arranging for extra counselors to come in to talk with students, and we have done some extra training for students in the peer counseling program."

"The moment of silence yesterday was nice," I say, sucking up to Dr. Albrecht.

"This is hard on everyone, but what makes it harder is people fighting about who was whose best friend, or things like that," Dr. Albrecht says, making sure to make eye contact with both of us. I hang my head in mock shame, while Brittney pretends to cry. I sense false tears.

"And people will feel guilty," I say as I admit to a new emotion, even as I accuse Brittney. "They'll wonder if Robyn would still be alive if they had done—or not done—something."

"That's a common reaction," Dr. Albrecht says. "That's why we want students who might feel that way to seek out counseling. Guilt is a common emotion linked with death."

I bite my tongue. In my house, Robyn's death was called "just wonderful" because death causes tears, and tears give us life. I know Brittney isn't one of us, but the crocodile tears she sheds for Robyn make me wonder. Brittney is treating Robyn's death as one more attention-getting opportunity.

"We need to get started," Mr. Abraham says. I sneak one more peek through the drawn curtain before we head out onstage. I see some people are laughing, some are already crying, but most just look stunned. It is the look of denial. The first stage of grief.

On every seat is a sheet of paper. The top of the page has a picture of Robyn and information about her life. The middle of the page contains information about the ceremony. The bottom of the page lists the five stages of grief to help everybody understand the grieving process.

I go out onstage along with Mr. Abraham, Principal Carlson, and Dr. Albrecht. There's a chair for Brittney, but she's still backstage. I turn around and go to her, speaking softly. "Brittney, it's okay. You can do this. All is forgiven. This is for Robyn."

"I can't," is all she says. Her voice isn't sad; it is angry for showing weakness in front of me. I don't gloat; instead, I lightly touch her arm, and pull her close.

"For Robyn," I say softly, and she nods. I give her my handkerchief, and she gives me a sad thank-you smile. She wipes her eyes, hands it back to me, and starts out onstage. Before I return, I press the handkerchief against my naked left shoulder, but feel no energy rush. The tears might be real, but the emotion behind them is false. One drop can energize me for weeks, but Brittney's tears so lack real emotional energy that I feel nothing. Just like Brittney. She's not upset; she's just trying to upstage everyone else by making a late entrance.

To the right of the podium is a large blowup of Robyn's junior picture. It is surrounded by collages of other photos printed from Robyn's Facebook page and from the yearbook. Mr. A asked the yearbook teacher, Mr. Kvasnica, to assist, so several students worked all night creating the collages. To the left of the podium are chairs for us, although one chair is missing—the chair we had originally set out for Craig, but his parents said he wouldn't participate in the memorial service. Looking out over the crowd, it seems as if he also couldn't bring himself to attend the services at all.

The adults all say how much everyone will miss Robyn and how everyone that knew her knows she would want people to be happy. Mr. Abraham says that the only way to heal is to first hurt and experience grief. He says people shouldn't feel embarrassed about weeping during the ceremony. Today, crying is a community ritual.

Brittney rises, slowly, when it is her turn. She looks out of place; all the teachers are wearing black with just small white flowers in their labels. Brittney's wearing her bright blue cheerleading uniform, but she can't show any enthusiasm. She gets six sentences into her speech, which Mr. A helped her write, and loses it. Everybody in the audience looks concerned.

I rush to the podium. "It's okay, Brittney," I tell her. But she's not looking at me; she's looking out at the audience looking up at her. I seek everyone's tears, but Brittney seeks their attention. I'm no better than she is. Both of us are using Robyn's death for our own selfish ends.

Mr. A helps her back to her seat, while I look at the crowd. Jocks who wouldn't cry if they broke a leg now sport quivering lips. Most of the girls don't even try to hold back. They obey Mr. A's words and are openly weeping. It's my turn to speak, and I've thought about this moment since I heard the news. I don't like speaking in public, so my words will be brief.

"I don't know what I can say that hasn't been already said here or said by all of you since you learned Robyn was gone," I say slowly. "We love you and miss you, Robyn. Good-bye."

The funeral tomorrow is for family and close friends only, so this is their chance to say good-bye. I want my actions, not my words, to speak for me. I nod to Michael, who is running the sound, and the music starts. While Robyn and I loved Beatles music, I needed something more current for the finale. Over the music I say, "On the bottom of the stage are boxes of flowers, a sign of hope and renewal. If you loved Robyn, come take a flower, bring it on the stage, place it in front of her picture, and say some final words to her. Like this song says, we have just memories, and they will never change."

Between the silence at the end of my speech and the first words of the songs by Fuel, there's a symphony of sorrow welling to a crescendo as "Leave the Memories Alone" starts.

One by one, Robyn's friends and closest classmates come up onstage to leave a flower by her photo. Some do it quickly, the way you'd pull off a Band-Aid, taking the pain all at once; others linger in front of the picture. Some are still in shock; most are in tears. I embrace all who invite it; some accept it and need me to shoulder their sorrow. Most people I know; a few—maybe seniors or sophomores—I don't. The few who stayed seated and laughed, I never want to know.

I notice three people not in attendance: Samantha, Scott, and Craig. I also notice the glares of hate from Kelsey, Tyler, and Cody. Cody's not alone; Kelsey's smug and smiling friend Bethany is with him. She's an athlete too; she runs track, obviously a sprinter. All four avoid me when they come onstage and pass by Robyn's photo. Even though the girls are crying, I don't reach out to them.

When Brittney sees them, however, she magically manages to pull herself together. The minute she walks onstage, her act goes away and her true self emerges. I knew when I touched her and soaked in her tears, she didn't feel grief or guilt. As Brittney stands in front of the photo of her dead friend, she pulls out her iPod to use as a mirror to fix her crocodile tears–stained makeup. Her friend is dead, and she's consumed not with sorrow or shame but with self-importance.

The song repeats twice before everyone has come up. Mrs. Carlson starts to speak, but I'm not listening. I'm thinking not about Robyn, but about myself. Memories may never change, but people change. I wonder if all creatures have it in their power to transform their very nature.

I focus again as Mrs. Carlson invites the school choir to come onstage. Tamika Ross, the best singer in the choir, starts slowly singing the oldie "Lean on Me" in the style of a gospel song. People who had sat down stand up when they hear it. After only two verses, anyone who had stopped crying has started again. People are holding hands, swaying back and forth, coming together as a community. As I walk toward some swimmer friends, two junior girls—Elizabeth and Sara—who sometimes ate lunch at Robyn's table, stop me. They were not her best friends, more like honors-class acquaintances, but maybe that's why they seem so emotional. They're crying, not because of memories, but I assume because they regret not knowing Robyn better.

I stand between Elizabeth and Sara, their hands intertwined with mine, their cascading tears falling on my bare shoulders as they listen to the song and lean on me. My body feels soaked, almost overfull, with all the emotional energy in the room. I'm feeling dizzy and disoriented, almost as if I am overdosing.

Sara tries to speak, but I let her know that now isn't the time to talk. It is a time to reflect. I look inside myself and damn not my deeds, but my very nature, which craves constant tragedy. My best friend is dead, but standing among this crying crowd, I've never felt so alive. Yet who—or rather *what*—I am has never felt so wrong.

NEWS REPORT #4

Police report that twelve-year-old Jason Hamilton of Midland returned home a few days ago after he was missing for almost a week. At this point, police are releasing few other details. In a related story, police reported six more incidents in the mid-Michigan area of elementary and middle-school boys being kidnapped, blindfolded, gagged, and then released after a few days. Previously thought to be isolated incidents, they are now all believed to be linked. In at least one other case, a black Ford van was seen nearby. In every case, the young person was walking alone. Police would only comment that they are puzzled by the cases, as these kidnappings have not involved ransom. One officer said anonymously that while sexual assault was not involved, the young men were "terrorized" but none suffered severe physical injury. The same officer noted, however, that "torture" occurred in each case.

CHAPTER 11

SATURDAY, MARCH 21

How are you doing, Becca?"

She looks up at me; her sad blue eyes look larger than ever. Her head's covered in a black scarf. It matches the black dress and the color everyone in her family wore this morning of mourning. Saint Dominic's was packed; Robyn would've loved to have been around so many people, even if they couldn't see her. The casket was closed, which didn't surprise me, but did sadden me.

Grandmother Maggie came with me, although she wasn't my first choice. I asked Scott, but he was working—waiting tables at Paul's Coney Island—and couldn't get time off. And he couldn't switch his work shift to later in the day because he has a hot date tonight. With me.

I wanted to sit with Becca at the funeral, hold her hand, give her strength, but Mr. Berry said his sister volunteered. The last thing he needed was a fight about funeral seating arrangements. But I'm next to her now, as people mill around the Saint Dominic's Family Life Center awaiting the repast. It's so odd for people to get together to break bread so soon after putting the closed casket into the cold hard ground. If anything proves the range of human emotion, it is a morning like this. From the anguish of the funeral Mass to the agony of the last ride to the cemetery to hearing laughter at this gathering of survivors, somehow humanity survives the depths of despair and always returns to hope. Like any species, humanity adapted this trait of emotional resiliency in order to survive.

Few people from school were invited; even fewer showed up. Someone—maybe it was me—made sure Mrs. Berry knew how Craig drove a nail through her daughter's heart with Brittney holding the stake, so neither one was invited. Several teachers attended, even Mr. Abraham, who wasn't one of Robyn's teachers.

Everybody's paying attention to Becca, so it's hard for me to comfort her, but there'll be time later. I've told her parents that unless I'm at the hospital, church, or school, I'll do my best to make myself available for Becca. I owe them; I know I can never tell them why.

"I want to go home," Becca says in between the steady stream of mourners paying their respects. She's sitting on a hard red plastic chair and looking as tired as the room's worn carpet.

"I wish I could take you," I say, kneeling down next to her. "This will be over soon."

"I don't know why we're doing this," she says, almost pouting. "It's weird."

"I know, but it is important for people to say good-bye," I tell her. "It's good they can gather together like this and share their sadness."

"Cass, can I ask you something?"

"Sure thing," I say, smiling brightly.

"Why do people cry?" she asks.

I try not to look at her strangely; there's already been too much of that today. As I've stood next to Becca, I've listened to people choosing their words as carefully as if they were navigating a minefield. The elephant in the room is an eight-year-old with cancer. Everybody knows that in the next year—two at most—they'll be back in this same room saying the same words, not *to* Becca but *about* her. Then, there'll be no surprise, but there'll still be as much sorrow.

"Cass?" Becca says, and I snap back to attention. "Are you going to answer my question?"

"I'm not sure," I say, as my eyes gaze out on the entire room. "Why do you think?"

"I think people cry when they're sad because when they're done crying, they don't feel as sad anymore. That's how I feel," she says, sounding too smart for eight. I think she asked me because she'd already thought about the answer. Like her sister, she's a little bit of a show-off.

"Maybe, Short Stuff. Maybe you're right." I'm still avoiding her wide eyes.

"To feel good, you have to feel bad," she says, and I finally look at her. She's beaming as if she's just won the spelling bee. She looks familiar; she looks like Robyn leading a cheer.

"That's so smart," I tell her, then pat her on the back.

"So why don't you cry, Cass?" she says very softly. "Don't you want to feel better?"

I look out over the room, desperately trying to find someone I know, but no one comes to my rescue. Instead, I'm left with Becca looking up at me, awaiting my answer.

"What do you mean?" I ask, stalling for time.

"I saw that you didn't cry for Robyn at the funeral this morning."

"Not everybody reacts the same way," I tell her, then sigh. "Everybody's different."

"That's what I thought," Becca says. She looks like she's about to ask me something else when another of Mr. Berry's sisters starts walking toward us and Becca yells, "Aunt Ella!"

"See you later, Short Stuff," I say, stealing a quick hug. "I'll be over tomorrow if I can."

"Okay, I'll miss you," she says, and proves it by hanging on tight. I get my face up next to her and give her a tiny kiss on the cheek. "I feel better when I cry. You should try it, Cass."

I rise, then start to walk toward the exit. The food's on the table in the Family Life Center, and all the tears have been shed in the church. Before Becca finds me again, I locate Maggie standing by the front door. She looks impatient, edgy. "Are you ready to go?" I ask.

"Yes," Maggie says. She's not looking at me; her eyes dart wildly around the room.

"Me too," I say. "I don't think I can take much more. I'm ready to explode."

"What did you say?"

"I said, Robyn was lucky," Scott says, his eyes for the first time not looking at me. We're at Coach's Pizza on a busy Saturday night.

"How could you say that?" I ask, then sip from my water bottle; Scott sips from his pop.

"To die like she did, fast and, except for probably a few seconds, painlessly," he says.

"You didn't come to her memorial," I say, pretending to pout.

Scott readjusts in his seat like a defendant on trial, then whispers, "I couldn't."

"It was hard for everybody," I say softly.

"But for her friends, her real friends like you, it must—," Scott starts, but stops when both of us hear loud laughing from a booth across the room. We look over to see Kelsey with Tyler, and Cody with Bethany. They've just noticed us; Cody hurls a hunk of bread across the room. It lands far short of the table; looks like Cody will be spending another baseball season on the bench.

"Immature assholes," I mutter.

"Do you want to leave?" Scott asks as he picks up the bread and puts it on our table.

"What do you think?" I ask.

"There are people waiting for tables," he says. "It's polite to go and let them sit."

I smile, ignoring another roll hurled our way. "That's so nice, Scott."

"Hey, this is what I do," he says. Earlier in the evening, Scott had told me funny stories about his job waiting tables, but also about how hard the work is. He sets down a nice tip along with the bill. I offer to pay as well, but he turns me down. I suspect, however, that will be the only time he turns me down this evening. Yes, he's kind, polite, and religious, but he's still a guy.

"Okay, but if we leave now, then they win," I say.

"We can't let the terrorists win," Scott says, then laughs. We've talked politics, current events, movies, and books. Unlike Cody, Scott reads the paper beyond the sports page.

I laugh, as I've done a lot this evening. Cody made me laugh by accident; Scott does it on purpose. As I watch Cody and his crew yak it up, I wonder how I stood him for a second, let alone six months. "Okay, we'll stay," I say, then smile. "What were we talking about?"

Scott pauses, bites his bottom lip, then mumbles, "I don't want to think about death anymore." We were talking about Robyn; but he's thinking about his grandmother. Scott and I left for our date from the hospital, a strange start to a beautiful evening.

"How is your grandmother?" I ask, unable to resist what comes naturally.

"Not much better," he says, looking down. "I know she's in pain, but she can't tell us."

"Do you know what you're going to do?" I ask.

"I overhear Mom on the phone. She needs full-time care and we can't afford it. Mom can't do it because she'd need to quit her job. I work all I can, but I can't quit school because then I'll never get into college," he says, then sighs. "It's a vicious circle, like life itself."

"What do you mean?" I ask.

"The whole thing about you're born helpless and sometimes, like my grandmother and my grandfather before her, you spend the end of your life equally as helpless. It's a circle."

"I'm so sorry."

He pauses, then once again finds his smile, a small, sideways one, but a smile nonetheless. "All we can do is pray to God that something will work out."

"Don't tell Samantha," I crack.

"She doesn't get it," he answers, then shakes his head in amusement and disgust.

"What do you mean?" I slide my hand another half inch closer to his.

His hands stay in place: one on the glass, one in his lap. "I don't want to talk about her."

"It's okay, Scott, whatever you want," I say, then pause to think how different Scott is from most guys I've met at Lapeer High. Most of my exes couldn't wait to speak badly of the girl who came before me. I wonder if the laughter at the other table comes from Cody cracking wise about me. Maybe he and Tyler are entertaining their dates with tales of the backseat. Whatever they're doing, it's causing a disturbance. I see their server speaking to them, but she's not getting anywhere. Her words are easily swallowed up into that ocean of assholes.

"Okay, but it's complicated," he says, showing he is open, but just needs a little prodding.

So I say, "Maybe you don't want to speak badly of the undead." He doesn't laugh.

"I guess I understand people like her," Scott says, then sighs. "They're afraid."

"Afraid of what?"

"Afraid of being themselves," he says. "That's why they adopt poses or join cliques."

"I don't know her that well," I say, although that might be changing. After the big door slam in the library and the eye knives in biology class, she's toned it down. I think her new thing is to act all mature, like she's above it. She surprised me by finally adding me as a MySpace friend, then also asking if she could interview me for the school paper about the peer

counseling service. Samantha thinks she'll be asking the questions; she obviously doesn't know me at all.

"I knew girls like her at Powers." He says the name of his
old school with a wince, like a bad memory. Not bad because
it was scary, but awful because it was good and now is gone.

"Well, there are a lot of them at Lapeer as well," I add. "I
try to avoid all the groups."

"I noticed," he says, almost whispering.

"I think she's like all of us, just trying to figure out who
we are," I say very casually.

"Well, she's got a lot more thinking to do," he says. "Like
the whole God thing."

"Not everyone believes in God like you and me."

He flashes a second of anger, but it melts when I offer my
best smile in return. This conversation is like a swimming meet
and I need to push ahead to the finish line.

"She *does* believe in God, she just hasn't put it all together."

"Scott, what do you mean?"

"Here's the story," he says, and I lean forward as if I'm
expecting a kiss. "An angel once found a demon broken and
nearly dead. The angel held out his arms to help the demon. The
demon looked at the angel and asked, 'Why would you save an
evil demon like me?' The angel answered, 'Because *without you,
there is no me.*'"

I'm smart, but I play dumb. "What do you mean?"

"If she really believes in vampires, then she believes in evil.
If she believes in evil, then she believes in demons. If she believes

in demons, she must believe in angels. If she believes in angels, then she believes in God," he says. "You don't get good without evil. They coexist."

"That's a rational explanation for the irrational, don't you think?"

"There's an order to things in the universe," Scott says, then finishes his pop.

"So do you believe in demons and vampires?" I ask, almost amused.

He lets out a small, almost embarrassed laugh. "Not like Samantha does, but, I guess I do."

"You're one interesting man, Scott Gerard," I say. My arms stretch out like I am trying to touch the wall of the pool. I can't reach out any farther to him; he's got to reach back.

"You too," he says, then touches me. "I mean, you're interesting, not an interesting man."

I think he's blushing, but I can't see all of his face. Instead, I feel his skin. "Thanks."

The moment's ruined by more yelps from Cody's table and another incoming bread bomb. I stare back at Cody, but he's not looking at me. They're too busy now throwing food at each other. I see the server walk by the table again, but that just sets off another laugh riot.

"I'm sorry, we should—," I start.

"I wanted to get to know you for some time," he says. "But I'd have to break my rule."

"Your rule?"

"Since pretty girls don't usually talk to me, I don't talk to them," he says as he blushes. "By talking to you, I'm breaking my rule. I wonder what other trouble you'll get me into?"

"Really?" I lean in. I want to push the hair out of his face; I want to see his eyes.

"I watched you, how you interacted with everybody at school," he says.

"Well, Robyn taught me that," I say.

"No, it was different," he says. "People clung to Robyn because it made them feel popular too, like they were part of something. But I think people hang around you because you make them feel better. I see how people talk to you when they're upset or crying."

"I try to be there for my friends."

"Robyn gave people what they wanted, you give people what they need," he says without a single pause, like he's been rehearsing this little speech for some time. "People worshipped Robyn, but people *like* you. I think that's probably better for everyone."

"Everyone except you liked me, I guess," I say, teasingly.

"I saw you with guys like Cody and couldn't figure you out," he says, pointing in their direction. I won't turn around. Not only because I don't want to look at Cody again, but also because I can't take my eyes off Scott. He's pushed his hair aside. If he blushes any more, there'll be no more blood left in the rest of his body, which would be disappointing for both of us later.

"Figure out what?" I ask. I'm fingering my trinity of necklaces with my left hand. My right hand flicks Scott's fingers. He looks up again. I throw back my hair and smile.

"Never mind," he says. Scott seems to be a mostly dormant volcano; he lets off a little steam, a little emotion, but I sense deep down there's more brewing and an explosion waiting.

"Scott, maybe you figured out that we belong together," I say as I lean closer.

"Really?"

"Really," I say, then squeeze his hand. "I think we can help each other."

"What do you mean?" he asks as our fingers awkwardly intertwine.

"My grandmother is head nurse at Avalon, this nursing home," I offer. "Let me talk with her, see what she can do to help your grandma. I'm sure she could pull some strings."

"You would do that?"

"Scott, of course I would," I say. "We have a lot in common."

"You think so?"

"You said how other people need me, but that's true of you too, Scott," I say, grasping his hand a little tighter. "Your family needs you."

"It's a lot to carry," he admits, but there's no way he could understand the cross I bear.

"Let me help you," I say, then let go of his hand. He looks surprised. I get up and move over to the seat next to him. "The first thing you should know is that we all need somebody to lean on."

He doesn't say anything as I whisper, "And the second thing I learned from Robyn. Maybe it's the last thing I learned from her."

"What's that?" he asks nervously.

I run my fingers gently but playfully through his hair. "You can't try to act strong all the time. It is too hard."

He doesn't say anything, but he turns to look at me. His green eyes flash "go."

"If you need to unload, if you need to cry or scream or shout . . . ," I say, then push against him. I take his hand from the table and put it near my waist. He clumsily wraps his arm around me while my body cries out silently for him to pull me closer. "If you need me, then I'm there."

He doesn't say anything because he's lost in my inviting eyes. "Scott, you didn't come to Robyn's memorial because you wanted to be strong." I gently tip his head against me. "You didn't want to cry, but you'll have to let it out. And when that time comes, I'll be there."

He stays silent, soaking it all in, and I wait to soak in his tears, but a laughter train headed our way breaks the silence. When Cody and his crew walk by our table, they laugh loudly as they knock over Scott's pop glass. It's empty, so only ice spills on the table.

"Just had to cool things off," Cody says as he walks past. Cody's crew cracks up.

"Apologize," Scott says as he stands.

Cody stops, turns around, and looks at Scott with disdain and shock. "What did you say?"

"I said, say you're sorry," Scott repeats. Cody, with Tyler at his side, walks back toward the table. Cody's got his varsity jacket on his shoulders and his jock pride on his sleeve.

"What are you going to do about it?" Cody sneers. They're nose to nose.

"Nothing," Scott says. It looks like he's trying not to smile. "Nothing, for now."

"Weirdo," Cody says. Tyler shakes his head in agreement, and they walk away.

"Scott, what are you doing?" I ask. "Do you know martial arts or something?"

"No," he says, sitting back down at the table. "No doubt, Cody would kick my ass."

"Then why—?"

"Because you can't allow that kind of behavior," Scott says, then rubs his forehead.

"But Cody and Tyler—"

"Brawn wins some battles," Scott says. "But in the end, brains always wins the wars."

I'm silent as Scott sits down next to me, and I wrap my arms around him. He leans into me, and after an awkward moment, I kiss him. I can tell he'll need lots of practice.

Scott breaks our awkward first real kiss quickly, then says, "We should go."

I'm confused, yet compliant. "Okay."

"The waitress needs this table," he says, then motions toward the server's area.

A tired-looking waitress comes over. Not our server, but the one who served Cody's table. Before she can say anything, Scott asks her, "They stiffed you, didn't they?"

The server isn't some high school girl; this is her job and her hard middle-aged life. She sighs, then says, "Yeah, and they left a mess too."

"Figures," he says. "On behalf of all Lapeer High School students, I apologize."

The server laughs, then says, "Thanks, it's okay."

"No, it's not," Scott says, not angrily, but with force. He reaches into his pocket, then pulls out a ten-dollar bill. He hands it to the server, then says, "Here's the tip they didn't leave."

"Are you for real?" the waitress asks.

Scott smiles his answer, but it looks like he wants to say something more. I want him to say, "I'm just falling in love," but he's not ready to admit that aloud, at least not yet. Not yet.

Scott leans over to kiss me, but instead I rush out the door. Like fire, I'm sucking all the air; as if human, I'm grasping for love. Scott comes up behind me and asks softly, "Cassandra, what's wrong?" then gently places his hand on my shoulder.

"Nothing," I say, knowing it is a total lie. For so long, I've told myself that if you can't feel love and don't mind being alone, then high school isn't that difficult. As I fall into Scott's open arms and his soft, loving glance, I sense that high school is about to become very, very hard.

CHAPTER 12

TUESDAY, MARCH 24

What do you want?"

My sneer is aimed at Kelsey, Brittney, and Cody's new squeeze, Bethany, all surrounding me at my locker. It's as if three Gap mannequins have cornered me.

"Do you have Robyn's Facebook password?" Kelsey asks. She's chewing her gum so hard and loud she looks like a cow with her cud. "It needs to go away."

"Why?" is my less-than-helpful response.

"Tomorrow will have been a week," Kelsey says. "Her Facebook profile reminds people . . ."

"So," I answer. I realize we'll all be counting weeks, not like most juniors who count the days until the end of the school year, but weeks since Robyn died. Tomorrow is week one.

"You took her boyfriend, now you want her life?" I ask Brittney. It seems Kelsey's the gum-filled mouthpiece. Brittney's silence indicates she's supervising this operation. Bethany's here just to gloat as if blond-haired, empty-headed Cody were a prize deserving of bragging rights.

"It's not about that," Brittney finally speaks. "It's about healing, and all that other stuff."

"I have to go," I say. "School's over for the day, and I'm done with the three of you."

"I didn't steal Craig," Brittney says, which stops my quick exit. "Craig dumped Robyn."

"If there's an unguarded vault and you take the money, it's still stealing," I counter. It's not my best argument, but I can't waste energy on them. "Especially, if you unlocked the door."

Kelsey steps forward, like the toady she is, in defense of Brittney. "It was bound to happen. Somebody was spreading rumors about Craig and Brittney. I wonder who did that?"

"I wonder. Perhaps, Kelsey, you should look beside you," I say. "Not in front of you."

"What do you mean?" Kelsey asks.

"Kelsey, don't act so dumb," I say. "It was Brittney who started the rumors herself." I have no idea if that's true or not. I'm throwing bread on the water to see if it floats her way.

Brittney grows quiet while Kelsey looks confused, so I'm probably right. "You ever heard of self-fulfilling prophecy?" I ask; she doesn't answer. "It was a sweet plan, actually."

"Shut up!" Brittney says.

"Brittney spreads the rumor. It drives a wedge between Craig and Robyn. Craig denies it, but Robyn doesn't believe

it. They fight, break up, and Brittney slips into Robyn's place."
I point a finger at Brittney's smug tanned face. "Also, Robyn
dies. You didn't count on that, did you?"

"You coldhearted bitch," Brittney says. "How did Robyn
ever hang out with you?"

"Because I cared about her," I say. "I didn't just use her."

"She just pretended to like you because of Becca," Brittney says. "I was her best friend."

"What are you, six years old?" I ask, then shake my head. "I
don't have time for this."

"Why? You have to go to church with Scott?" Kelsey cracks.

"What is wrong with you?" Brittney asks. "To go from Cody
to a loser like Scott."

Kelsey laughs on command. "So, are you going to give
Brittney the password?"

"No."

"Then you're *dead* at this school. We'll see to that," Brittney says.

"I don't care," I calmly say. "I have all the friends I need."

Brittney laughs, then says, "Scott and Samantha Dracula—
some friends."

"Her name is Samantha Dressen," I say. I don't add that
she's still not a real friend. Yet.

"It's a freak show," Brittney says, and Kelsey and Bethany
giggle almost on command.

"You three are ones to talk about a freak show," I snap
back as Kelsey snaps her gum.

"What do you mean?" Brittney says.

"You're all ridiculous, with your fake orange tans, your slutty tight clothes, and your always-open legs," I say. I've wanted to say these things for a long time, but held my tongue. Robyn counted Brittney as one her best friends for some odd reason. Since Robyn didn't get a chance to reject her, I'll do that task with pleasure. "You're the freaks, not me or Scott."

"Hey, maybe if you opened your legs, you'd still have Cody," Kelsey says. I can't tell if Bethany looks embarrassed or excited. The only look Cody will ultimately give her is disappointment.

"Maybe if Robyn didn't act like a prude, Craig wouldn't have left her," Brittney says.

"Maybe if you had kept you legs shut for Craig, then Robyn would still be alive," I say, proving I'm as cold as they claim.

"Bitch," Brittney says, then pushes me. As I've always learned, I turn the other cheek—but not before I laugh.

"You are so dead," Brittney says with another push.

"No, that's Robyn who is dead," I say, still stone-cold. "And you pulled the trigger."

Out of words, Brittney resorts to violence with another push. I swat her hands away, then stare her down. This isn't the evil eye of a teacher. I learned this stare not from a Lapeer wigger or wannabe, but from bangers in NOLA. This is a real deal "don't fuck with me" gangsta glare.

I keep my violet pupils poised like laser beams on Brittney, then whisper, "Just try me."

"What makes you think you're so tough?" Brittney asks, and the question is the answer.

"I'm not so tough, Brittney," I say as she blinks. "For all your attention-getting antics, you know what you are?" I don't give her time to reply. I fix my stare even harder, then say, "You're a weak, spoiled, selfish little girl." Brittney quickly focuses on the floor instead of the anger in my eyes and the truth in my words. All three quickly exit. Their high heels click in time.

"So, Samantha, what do you want to ask us?" I say, and Mr. Abraham marks his approval with a sip from his thermos. He and I are sitting in a small conference room in the library after school. Samantha Dressen in all her human-hating vampire-loving glory sits across from us. Skulls cover her notebooks, red ink covers her hands, and long sleeves cover her arms. Her hair is tinted green, at least for today.

"I'm writing an article for the school paper on the peer counseling service," she says, but I sense she's got another agenda. Just like I do. We have something else, other than Scott, in common it seems. "With recent events—"

"I love your poems on your MySpace," I say, cutting her off, not angrily, but faking excitement. I'd printed one earlier and showed it to her. It's called "I Hurt, Hurt, Hurt" just like her screen name, and I suspect, like her life. In the poem, she writes about having no more tears, but I know that's a lie.

"This is just something for the paper," she mumbles.

"How long have you been writing?" I ask, then sip from my water bottle.

"Since I've been writing," she says, then cracks what looks like a smile.

"I'd like to read more," I say, then lean toward her. "I really would."

She nods, but I think she wants to shout. This is what you do to make friends; you tell people things they want to hear. I really don't want to read Samantha's emo-laden odes to her anguish, but I do want to learn about the person behind the words. It's another of my sacrifices.

"How long have you been writing for the paper?" I ask.

"Just this year," she says, almost in a mumble.

"I'll have to go back and look at some of your stories. Which one is your best?"

"I guess the story about the Goth tree," she says. All the Goth kids used to hang out by this small tree by the parking lot. People called it the Tree of Doom and Gloom. Somebody chopped it down over Thanksgiving break. The Goths blamed the jocks, the jocks blamed the stoners, and the stoners blamed the preps. For days, the school overflowed with drama going on between the groups. "I wish I could have found out who did it. Do you know?" she asks.

"I'll ask around for you," I say, all cool and calm. "Is that okay?"

"Thanks, Cassandra," she says like she's lost in a fog.

"Cass," I say.

"Samantha, did you have some questions for us?" Mr. A asks, sounding much annoyed.

"So, about the peer counseling service, how long has it been going on?" she asks.

I stay silent, so Mr. A takes over telling the story of how I came to him in the spring last year and suggested that students needed a safe place to talk about their problems with people who could understand. He goes into detail—he's a science teacher and prone to give way too much information—about what we do and how many students we've helped. All the while, I'm looking at Samantha. She's more of a puzzle than a person. Ever since that day in class when she spoke up about not believing in God, I've tried talking with her, but she's been resisting. We've made an online connection, but it is a long way from a friendship. She doesn't know that I suggested this story to the newspaper editor and asked that she write it.

"Did Robyn ever talk to—," Samantha starts, but I cut her off.

"I'm sorry, but that's confidential, Samantha," I say sharply, but with a smile to cover my rudeness. "Every student needs to know what they tell us will never, ever leave the room."

"Then how do you explain all the gossip?" she says, trying to act the part of reporter.

"Because it's high school," I say, then laugh.

Samantha laughs too, probably out of nervousness, then

says, "So true." Samantha is not a source or spreader of gossip; rather, she's a subject for rumors about every aspect of her life.

"The hardest thing for people is admitting they need help," I say with cold calculation.

Mr. A nods and tells Samantha more about the service. As she writes, she's looking at her notebook, not at Mr. Abraham. Most days in class, that's her style. Head down, not asleep, but certainly not engaged. No eye contact. Mr. A pauses after he mentions Robyn's death.

"Don't write this," I tell Samantha. "But most people never heard about or used the peer counseling service until Robyn died. Be honest, had you ever heard about it?"

Samantha shakes her head so she doesn't have to speak a lie. I know she made two appointments and no-showed both. She's aware, interested, but like many students, too afraid.

"The students are not professionals, but we give them tools to help students going through a difficult time," Mr. Abraham says in a tone that I imagine a proud father would use.

"Like this." I pull out a small pamphlet from my bag. "It's the stages of grief."

"Stages of grief?" she asks.

"Denial, anger, bargaining, depression, and then acceptance," I rattle off, then hand the brochure to Samantha. "It's by a woman named Elisabeth Kübler-Ross. You can keep it."

He nods again, then tells Samantha more about how well the school as a whole handled Robyn's death. I didn't see Samantha at Robyn's memorial service. I need to know why.

"Cassandra, anything else you want to add?" Mr. Abraham asks.

"Maybe later. I hope this helped," I say. Mr. Abraham smiles at me, then offers his good-byes to both of us, and exits. He and I will talk more about this later at the pool. I gather up my heavy bag, but before I can exit, Samantha asks, "How did you do that?"

"Do what?" I reply.

"I was supposed to interview you, but somehow you ended up asking me questions."

"I'll answer more questions if you have them," I say, and she starts flipping through her notebook. She starts to speak, but I cut her off. "I have a better idea."

"What's that?"

"You want to be a writer, don't you?" I ask, but she doesn't answer.

"Not just for the school paper, but write books?" Again, she doesn't answer.

"I read when writing exposition you shouldn't tell, you should show," I say as the noose tightens. "Let me show you what peer counseling is like. Come in for a session."

"I don't think so," she says, slamming her notebook shut. If it were a door, the hinge would have broken. "No offense, Cassandra—I mean Cass—but you can't handle my shit."

"Just try me," I say, but there's softness in my eyes and voice. It's an offer, not a dare.

"I'm sure Scott told you everything anyway," she says, then gets up to leave. When she bends over for her bag, I snatch her notebook. I leaf through it hyperquick. There's page after page of poetry, mostly written in small letters in red ink. There are drawings on many of the pages, lots of coffins, crosses, razor blades, and roses. "Give that back!" she shouts.

"Samantha, you have so much to say; talk to me," I say, handing back the notebook. When I pass it to her, a piece of paper falls out. It is the paper from Robyn's memorial service. I touch her wrist with my free hand, then whisper, "You were there."

"Look, I have to go," she says, but my hand now clutches her long black sleeve.

"I looked for you there," I say. "Where were you hiding?"

"I have to go," she repeats, but she's not moving.

"Samantha, it's okay to be upset. It's okay to let it out."

She takes the paper from my hand, then shakes her head. Her long black and green hair falls in her eyes. She pulls out some cheap MP3 player and puts in her buds to drown me out.

"When you're ready to talk," I say, my voice escalating to match the speed metal band now shouting in Samantha's ears. Words may not be enough, so I'm mulling a drastic act.

"You wouldn't understand!" she shouts.

"Try me!" I shout back.

"No," is all she says, but I notice what she does: she turns down the music.

"You can't do this," I say firmly. "Friendship isn't MySpace. Life isn't about vampires. This is real shit you are living. I get that. Just tell me. Let me help so you can heal."

"Fuck you!"

"You think this helps?" I grab her arm with one hand and pull up the sleeve with the other. There are more crosses on her arms than are found in most churches.

She gets her arms free, takes a step back, then rips the buds out of her ears.

"You don't know what it's like being me," she says, her voice choking with an emotional thunderstorm of rage, sadness, and desperate longing. It's all thunder, but no rain, no tears.

"Why do you say that?" I ask, then motion her to sit back down. She obeys.

"Everybody likes you," she says, pulling down her sleeve.

"Not true," I correct her.

"Nobody hates you."

"Wrong again."

"Never mind."

"What do you want to say?" I ask, toning it down. "What's *your* story, Samantha?"

She stares at me, in me, through me, and out the other side. Her eyes are not wet with tears; they are red with rage. "You're not an outsider like me. How could you understand?"

"Everybody's different."

"You don't understand! Nobody fucking understands a fucking thing about me!"

"I understand more than I can tell you," I say, then mutter "shit" under my breath.

"I don't believe you," she says, now sounding tired, defeated, yet still defiant.

Soft won't work on her; her walls are too hard, so I yell, "You don't believe in anything!"

She starts to say something, then pulls it back. She clutches the sheet of paper and then places it back in her notebook of sorrow-filled psalms. Somebody knocks on the door, but neither of us turns around. For a girl who rarely makes eye contact with others, Samantha stares at me without flinching. Just as a medical examiner looks over a corpse, her eyes travel over every inch of me. There's another knock at the door. Samantha breaks her stare to turn around and flip off the two goofy-looking boys standing by the door.

"I believe you now," she whispers, but I don't respond.

"I was at Robyn's ceremony," she says. "I sat in the back. I kept my head down so nobody could see me, but I saw you. I watched you. I watched you the day after she died too."

"This is about you," I say as the urge to flee overwhelms me. I grab the doorknob.

"And you never cried. You never shed a single tear for your good friend."

I turn the knob a notch.

"Brittney, Kelsey, Bethany—they all cried, but not you. Not you."

I stop, as if time had frozen this instant.

"I see how kind you are to people and just now, how you've made me—*me*—open up to you even though we're not really friends," she says, and I want to disappear. "By all rights with you dating my ex, we should be enemies. But I won't let that happen."

"Good."

"Do you know why?" she asks.

"Probably because you seem more mature than most other people and you—"

"There you go again." She cuts me off. "You turned this back on me. It's about you."

"I just thought you might want someone to talk to, that's all."

"I don't need your pity, but it's something else," she whispers. "It's not natural."

"It's just the way I am," I say, then sigh. "I'm curious and I like to help. It's my nature."

"No, this is different. It's almost supernatural," she whispers even softer.

"Don't go Goth on me," I say, but she takes out a mirror. She stares at my reflection in it, even as I pull out the cross around my neck, then joke, "Do you want me to eat some garlic?"

"You knew all the things to say to get me to open up," she continues, while I try to stare her silent. "I know you do this peer counseling so people can tell you their secret pain."

"I do it to help people," I say, trying to sound credible.

"Cassandra, I do believe you," she says slowly, each word pounding like a nail in my hands.

"Believe what?" I say with one foot out the door.

"That you *do* know what it's like to feel different from everyone else. And I know why."

I take a step back inside, then close the door hard, and look at her even harder. "Why?"

"You're not like everyone else, Cassandra, and I know your secret." I pull in my breath and hold it as if I were underwater as Samantha whispers, "It's because you're not human."

CHAPTER 13

WEDNESDAY, APRIL 8

*A*re you sure?"

"Of course, Cass," Scott says, then smiles at me. We're bathed in beautiful early spring twilight and sitting on the bumper of Scott's car parked out at the Holly Rec area. We've spent most of our time in the car, mainly in the back-seat, but we've come up for air.

"I'd love to go to prom with you," I say. It's not much of a lie. Proms and the like don't mean anything to me, other than that they're often ripe for high-pitched high school drama.

"It won't be fancy," he says, sounding ashamed. "We'll be in my no-volt Cobalt rather than some limo."

"I bet my mom could help," I say, although that's wishful thinking.

"I'll find the money," he says. "I will work for your love."

"What did you say?" I ask, pretending not to hear, trying not to shout, desperately aching inside with conflicted feel-ings. The feelings themselves are the conflict.

"Nothing," he says, sounding like a totally different person. "I hate limos."

"I don't need a limo. I just want whatever you want," I say, staring into his suddenly sad eyes. There was a limo for Robyn's funeral, just like there was one for Scott's grandfather. I imagine he's wondering if his next limo ride will be to the prom or to the cemetery.

Scott finds his smile, then whispers like he doesn't want to be heard, "I do love you."

I want to reply with those same words, but I've said them before to the Codys of the world. I've never meant it, not once. I only want to say it again when it's *not* a lie. But I must say something: "Scott, you're so sweet."

Scott looks more confused than sad. "I shouldn't have said that," he says.

"Don't take it back." I'm wondering what took him so long to say those three words.

"I'm sorry," he says. "I don't want to mess this up."

I'm silent again, focusing my energy on shutting down this tingling in my body. I've never felt it before, so I can't name it. It's a feeling no one in my family could understand, except Siobhan; a feeling as forbidden as the apple in Eden. All I can do is enjoy the ride, wherever it takes me. I speak with actions, not words, and kiss Scott on the mouth, sucking his bottom lip.

This is how I've spent the last two and a half weeks: attached to Scott's lips. While I go to school, volunteer at the hospital,

and do peer counseling, Scott is what matters. I still see Becca;
I need her as much as she needs me. We talk about Robyn. It
makes us feel good, even if Becca does cry. I'm making progress
with Samantha, but Scott commands my attention. I find myself
smiling for no reason, but, of course, there's a reason. He's
attached to my lips.

"You're sure you want to go?" he says when we break the
kiss. Like Samantha, it seems that Scott almost invites rejection. No wonder they came together; no wonder it didn't last.

"If that's what you want, Scott."

"I knew you'd say that," he says, stifling a laugh. "What
do you want, Cass?"

I'm stuck because Scott's so unlike all my exes. He's not
stuck on himself and his own wants. It's true now sitting on
the bumper of his car; and it was true in the backseat.

"I want whatever you want," I whisper.

"I want to know what you want," he whispers back.

"Scott, I want you."

"I just want to be happy for once," he says, then sighs.
"God, I hate when I whine."

"It's okay, Scott. Everybody hurts. Didn't Samantha teach
you—"

"Please don't make fun of her," he says, sounding hurt himself, even vulnerable. I move closer, ready to take advantage,
but I can't do it. It's like I'm playing a video game and my con-
troller is broken. I know what to do and say, but I can't pull the
tear-inducing trigger.

"That's so nice that you don't talk badly about her," I say instead.

"It just didn't work out," he says, then mumbles, "She wasn't my type."

"Really?" I ask with an arched eyebrow. "So who is your type?"

He pauses, then says, "Someone like you."

I don't know what to say; I only know what to do, so we kiss again.

After I break the kiss, Scott says, "The thing is that Samantha's very complicated."

"I don't know her that well."

"That's what I want."

"What?"

"I want you to know Samantha better. Be her friend."

"I want to know her better, but she doesn't like me," I say. I feel vulnerable around her, but I can't admit that to Scott, and barely to myself. She doesn't know about me, I tell myself. Like so many rumors, her "you're not human" statement was a guess. A guess she got right.

"Give her a chance," he says. "Make peace with her. Become her friend."

I don't tell him that I'm already working toward that goal. "Can I ask you something?"

He nods, and I ask, "Why do you want me to do this?"

He leans closer. "I'll tell you something, but you can't tell anyone."

I try not to lick my lips. "Don't tell anyone" are the most seductive syllables ever.

"She said she was afraid that when the yearbook gets published, she wouldn't have anybody to sign it," Scott says, sounding very sad. "It's sad to see someone so lonely."

"What about all her Goth friends?"

"Are all the people we go to church with our friends?" he asks. Scott and I went to church together last Sunday. He's the only guy I know who considers going to Mass a date. "Believing in the same things and believing in each other, well, it's not the same."

"You'll need to help me," I say, sealing the deal with a kiss. This is another tightrope I'm used to walking: getting people to reveal themselves while keeping myself hidden. It's almost never a problem with guys, even rarely with girls. Samantha already thinks she knows something about me, so I'll need to make it all about her. The best way to do that isn't always to get people to talk about their problems; the best way is to get them talking about their dreams.

"I'll do anything for Samantha. I feel bad for her," he says. And I know he means it.

I just smile at Scott; he's the anti-me, filled with raw empathy and complex emotions. He's everything I'm not. It's not that he's my polar opposite; he's the other half of the circle.

"I'd better get home," he says, and then starts walking us back to the car. As he opens the door for he me, he says, "I've never done this before."

I look oddly at him. There's a lot Scott's doing for the first time with me, although not as much as past boyfriends. His strong faith and fumbling inexperience seem to hold him back.

"I've never lied to Mom about where I was going," he says.

"These are not normal times," I say, trying to reassure him.

"This isn't easy for me," Scott says. "I have certain beliefs, but around you—"

A kiss cuts him off. He doesn't know it's not my faith, but my nature, being challenged.

"You'll call Samantha, right?" he says as we move inside the car. He finds a scrap of paper on the Cobalt's messy floor, then writes down her cell number.

"As soon as I get home," I say, which is only a minor lie. The bigger lie when I get home will be explaining where I've been to my family, who can't know about Scott.

Scott kisses me one last time before we drive back toward my house. Along the way, we listen to Beatles songs from Robyn's iPod as I rest my head on Scott's shoulder. As the epic, almost symphonic, sounds of John Lennon singing "Across the Universe" wash over us, something else is washing over me. And if I'm not careful, it might just wash me away.

"Thanks for meeting me," I tell Samantha. We're sitting at the Tim Hortons donut shop down the street from me. It's mostly old guys who don't quite know what to make of Goth Girl and

Swimmer Chick. Their tired midnight-hour eyes examine us like rubberneckers passing a car accident.

"Any excuse to get out of my house." She sips her coffee. Bitter black, nothing sweet. Like herself, like her outfit. Dressed as always in black, Samantha's a daily funeral procession.

"I feel bad that we've had trouble between us," I confess. "I'm sorry."

"Sorry for dating my ex?" she asks. "Or sorry for making fun of me?"

"Samantha, listen, I've never made fun of you. But let me say, I'm sorry if you think I did. Other than Scott, I think we have a lot in common. I'd really like us to be friends."

"Really?" she asks. Her eyes pierce me through her thick black eyeliner.

"I thought about being a writer," I say, trying not to lock eyes. "But I don't know now."

She sips some more coffee; she bites some more bait. "Why's that?"

"Because you're already so good, compared to me."

"Bullshit," is her unexpected response. Her defenses are layered like her clothes, with one shirt piled atop another. "Just knock that shit off and tell me what you really want."

"Why do you assume that—?"

"Cassandra, everybody wants something," she says. Her MySpace profile lists her as bi, so I'm wondering what she wants from me, and how far I'll go to get what I need from her.

"What do you want then, other than to be a writer?" I ask, then sip from a bottle of water.

"I want you to talk to me like a person, and stop asking me all these questions," she says. "I'm not some guy you're trying to make out with. Just be a normal person, okay?"

"Just like you," I say with the best smile I can summon at midnight in a Tim Hortons.

"You got me," she says, then laughs. When she laughs, her facade momentarily fades.

"Okay, I'll make you a deal," I say, then flash quickly to my family. The only way to "deal" with the world is to make deals. "No more probing peer counseling questions from me."

"Good, thank you," she says.

"In return, you need to stop saying strange things like what you said to me the other day," I say, tapping the table for emphasis. "I'm like any other person. Nothing more, nothing less."

She laughs, smiles, then says, "You doth protest too much."

My fake smile vanishes as I say, "I'm serious."

There's silence at the table as we stare each other down again. I suspect her motive for knowing me better is to fulfill her vampire fantasies; my motive is darker—keep your enemies closer than your friends. I'll let her into my world just enough to keep her from the truth.

I break my stare and frown. She laughs, then says, "I guess we can't fight our natures."

"What do you mean?" I ask, unable to break my question-asking addiction.

"I mean however or whoever you are, I guess you can't change all that much," she says. She's staring at the old donut eaters who are staring at me. "I'll always be this way. I can change my clothes, my hair, all of that stuff on the outside, but I can't change my basic nature."

"Maybe," I say, thinking that mainly what I want to change is the conversation, so I add, "You have a great sense of humor, and . . . " It's pitch-black outside, but I stop speaking with a blinding-light revelation. *I don't know how to talk to people.* I can flirt with boys, ask questions of strangers, and help other girls with their problems. But I don't know how to have a simple, genuine conversation like a normal human being. She's right; my nature is that I'm abnormal.

"And?" she asks. She's not asking for flattery, just for me to finish my thought.

"And nothing," I say. "Just that I think you have a sense of humor, that's all."

"Scott was funny too," she says, then sips her coffee. "Let's get this out in the open."

I nod, then sit up in my seat. She leans in closer; her clothes smell of stale smoke.

"Scott and I broke up for lots of reasons, none of which I want to talk about," she says, struggling with words. This conversation resembles a baby's awkward yet excited first steps.

"I don't need to know, that's okay," I reassure her.

"I need to say this. I was mad at you. I'm sorry for that day in the library." I give her a sympathetic "it's all good" nod, so she continues. "Then it hit me. I liked Scott. If you like somebody, you want them happy. If being with you makes him happy, then that's what's best."

"That's mature." I don't say that it's because Scott feels the same that I'm sitting here.

"That's real life," she says, then takes her final sip of coffee.

"You want some more coffee?" I ask.

"Sure, where else do I have to go?" she cracks.

"I avoid my house all I can too." I take the cup from her. It's smudged with auburn lipstick. "You see, we *do* have a lot in common."

As I get up to get more coffee for her, and another bottle of water for myself, I sneak a peek at my phone. There are several messages from Mom, but even more from Scott.

When I get back to the table, Samantha says, "Can I ask you something?"

"Sure," I say as I sit back down.

"Did you ever find out for me who chopped down the Goth tree last fall?"

I pause, take a sip from my water bottle, then say, "No. Why do you ask?"

"You act like you know everything about everybody," she says.

"Maybe."

"Well, except you don't know shit about me, but that's for another day," she says.

"Is that a promise or a threat?" I ask, then laugh.

"It's whatever you want it to be," she says in a nervous, almost flirting, voice.

"I'll let you know what I find out."

"Once you find out, would you mind if I use it?" she asks in an embarrassed tone.

"Use what?"

"The thing about the Goth tree," she says, hiding a smile. "It's for a book I'm writing."

"You're writing a book? Tell me about it," I say. She smiles as she swallows the hook.

Samantha drops me at home an hour later. We're breaking the law, as well as the rules of both our houses, but we don't care. I give her a simple good-bye wave, then walk as quietly as possible into the house. Samantha doesn't help my stealth entrance by blasting death metal from her beat-up Honda as soon as she pulls out of my driveway. I learned a lot about Samantha tonight, and even more about her epic vampire fantasy. But mostly, I think how out of place she is at school and how awkward our conversation was. No wonder she wants to believe in vampires; like her, they don't fit in with the human race. No wonder we're becoming friends.

I check my cell as I climb the stairs up to my bedroom.

There's another message from Scott, and one from my cousin Lillith, whom I'll see at the reunion on Friday. She's calling to make plans; she must be forgetting that plans have already been made for me. I get online and check the weather for the weekend. The forecast is for mostly clear blue skies. But I check my news alerts and know, for me, there is nothing in store except heavy black clouds.

NEWS REPORT #5

Police have now confirmed that the series of child abductions in mid-Michigan is the work of the same person. While police are holding back many details due to the age of the victims, it is clear that one person—the gender is still unknown—has abducted eight male children in the area over the past six months. In each case, the young person was walking home alone. They were attacked and then dragged into a van. Inside the van, the young people were blindfolded and gagged. The police have yet to release more information other than that they allude to the "bizarre" details of the case. One police source said that the young people were not only "terrorized" by their abductor, but in several cases, they were also physically injured.

CHAPTER 14

THURSDAY, APRIL 9

*S*cott, I'll see you at school, okay?"

Scott's just asked if he could drive me to school, but I gently refused him. Unlike Cody, who couldn't handle the smallest rejection, Scott takes it in stride.

"It's complicated," I explain slowly. "But you can't meet my family; not yet."

"I guess I understand," he says.

"Good, because I sure don't!" I crack back and he laughs. "That's just the way it is."

"Are you the black sheep or something?" he asks.

"That's not me," I reply, jokingly, but my thoughts turn serious. There is a black sheep in our family, and with the reunion tomorrow, I've thought for days about calling Siobhan again. She's of my generation, but she won't be at the reunion this year, or ever again. To me she's a curiosity, but to the family she's an outcast.

"You there?" Scott asks. He's not used to my awkward pauses and mind ramblings. Our edges are still rough, no matter how much we rub our mostly clothed bodies together.

"Sorry, I got lost," I confess.

"Then it's a good thing I found you," he says and I feel my body sway.

"Well, I've just been waiting for you," I snap back.

"That's life, you know?" he asks, then sighs. "It is all one big waiting room."

"Really?"

"You sit and wait for something to happen," he continues. "Sometimes it's good, sometimes it's bad. And then, like you, sometimes it's great."

"So you don't need to spend your time in a waiting room anymore!"

"Right, but because of you," he says, then laughs, "I spend more time in confession."

"Sorry," I reply, although I'm not.

"Well, I don't drink, smoke, do drugs, or swear," he says. "Nobody's perfect . . . well, nobody except you, Cass."

I pretend to purr before I hang up and start walking to school.

It is a beautiful morning, thick with fog. It's a long, lonely walk to school, but it feels so good to soak up all the damp, dewy air. The dry winter air damages my skin. I didn't think

there was enough moisturizer in the world, and even a humidifier in every room of our house hasn't helped much. School is
even worse, with old-time heaters drying out my skin like an
oven.

On this morning, none of that matters. Just as I spoke in Bio
about the space between faith and fact, this morning I'm thinking about the space between family and friends, between loyalty
and love. These are tightropes I thought I knew how to walk.
I thought wrong. These are not questions I can ask Mom,
Grandma Maggie, and especially not Veronica. There's only
one person who could understand. Just outside of school, I sit
on a curb and make the call.

"Siobhan?" I ask the female voice who answers.

"Hello?" She sounds confused. Or maybe just asleep. It's
still predawn in California.

"It's Cassandra," I say.

"Cassy, I told you not to call me again," she says. "I'm out
of the family."

"I need to talk to you," I whisper.

"I can't talk," she says. "It's for your own good."

"I don't care." The outside fog soothes me; my inner fear
drives me. "We used to be close, you can't turn me down. That
wouldn't be the human thing to do, would it?"

She coughs and considers, then says, "Okay, one last time.
What's wrong?"

"You know what weekend it is, don't you?" I ask. For

most people in Lapeer, this weekend is an excuse to send
Easter cards, eat chocolate, and paint eggs. For my family, it's a
chance to come together to remember and reenact our family's
history and heritage.

"Yes. I know you and Alexei are of age," she says. She's
always been my favorite cousin; no wonder Veronica frets over
me. She's afraid I'll be like Siobhan and abandon my ancestors.

"I can't live like this anymore," I say.

"I *felt* exactly the same way," she says, and the word shocks
me. In my family, speaking of feelings is forbidden. Instead, we
talk about loyalty, honor, and duty. It is more like the Mafia
than a family. And Siobhan learned what happens when you go
against the family.

"I've met this boy, Scott," I say. "He's like nobody else."

"So is Alden," she says. Alden is her boyfriend; Alden is
the cause of her exile.

I pause and look around me. I see buses, cars, and SUVs
turn into the school parking lot. I see people walking or biking.
Everybody, it seems, is with someone. They're connected. Like
Siobhan, I'm in exile. But my exile is from emotion, normality,
and most of all, from humanity. Until Scott. Now there's a tingling, like a body part that's fallen asleep but is coming awake.

"Cassy, are you okay?" she asks.

I pause again, take in the world I know, compare it with
the world I want, and say, "No."

We talk for another ten minutes as I pour out these growing

human feelings of love, and even sadness. We keep talking but Siobhan never reveals—despite my best efforts—how she left the family. As I'm about to hang up, I ask one last question. "Siobhan, are you happy?"

"Cassy, I'm very happy," she says without pause or hesitation.

"What does that feel like to be happy, to be in love?" I ask.

"I can't describe it," she says. "You have to experience it for yourself."

"How will I know I'm really in love?" I ask.

"Love exists between natural and supernatural," she says, speaking words Mom should have spoken to me. "It is a mystery you take on faith."

"But Siobhan, I need to know how you become fully human once you feel *love*. How—"

"In the family, we don't use the word, but all the sacrifices you make for the family is what love looks like," she says. "When you're willing to lose everything for someone else, that's what love looks like." Her soft words scream in my ears, almost drowning out the school bell. As I say good-bye, I wonder when my faith will be rewarded and the mysteries solved.

"Mr. Abraham, can I say something?"

"Cassandra, what would you like to add?" Mr. A asks as Honors Biology winds up. It's the first class in the last day

before my personal spring break starts. Although I know he tries
to avoid it, his tone makes me sound like the teacher's pet.

"Maybe both evolution and creation are right. Why does it
have to be one or the other?" I ask the class, earning a frown
from Mr. A and serious sighs from other students. For most of
the class, I've been my silent self, but Siobhan's words stir inside
me like a boiling cauldron.

"What do you mean?" some girl behind me asks.

"Maybe Adam and Eve are just names for the first fully
evolved humans," I say.

"Not Koko and Lucy, those talking apes," somebody says.

"No, the talking apes are all in gym class," Scott cracks.
He gets mostly laughs, but he's playing to a friendly house.
I'm the only athlete in the room; nobody else in this class has
the anatomy, coordination, or ambition.

I laugh, even if the joke is at my expense, although I'm not
sure Scott realizes that. For all the rules of science I've studied,
there's one sure rule for maintaining chemistry in a relationship:
laugh at your boyfriend's jokes. With Tyler and Cody, that took
better acting skills than the finest actors in our school, but with
Scott, it's easy. When he's not feeling down about his grandmother, he's full of life, and I overflow with appreciative and
genuine laughter.

Mr. A lets the class go off into discussion, sometimes playing
devil's advocate. I drop out of the conversation again to think
about Siobhan's words and gaze upon Scott's face.

"Well, if God invented everything, why did he invent diseases like AIDS and cancer?" Michael asks, and I stir in my seat. Though I spent so much time with Becca right after Robyn's death, it's been weeks since I've visited. It's not just Scott, but it's my family—in particular, Veronica—driving us all crazy with details about the reunion. For me, spring break starts a day early, since our school doesn't let us out for Good Friday, the holiest of holy days in our family.

I tune back in to the discussion every now and then, but my mind is far away until I hear somebody make a crack about monsters. It's a comment meant to bait Samantha and it works.

"Don't call something you don't understand a monster," Samantha says.

"Freak," Clark Rogers mutters.

"Shut up!" I say, defending Samantha to Clark, but also offering her a smart suggestion.

I sink into my seat as Samantha ignores my advice. "You use the word 'monster' for any creature, any nonhuman being, that you don't understand or accept. I accept them all," she says.

Lots of hands go up, which is no surprise. It's one thing to fill your MySpace page with vampire lore; it's another thing to talk about it in class in front of skeptical science students.

Samantha stands her unholy ground as others attack. She's all alone, until Scott raises his hand. "Samantha, you said you didn't believe in God."

"I don't." She's looking at him with a pierced and arched eyebrow.

"But isn't God supernatural as well?" Scott says. "So you can accept God. Anyone who accepts Christ, Mohammad, or Buddha accepts there are things beyond science. It's logical."

Samantha stares at Scott; it looks like she's not angry but appreciative. She mouths the word "thanks," and he smiles back in her direction. A normal person might be jealous. I'm not.

"So what about AIDS?" Michael asks. "I don't understand why science or God would create such a disease."

A few people in the room start to talk. Mr. Abraham guides the discussion, but doesn't offer fact or opinion. There are plenty of questions, but no answer. It's my turn.

"AIDS, like any disease, is probably a necessary mutation," I say with confidence.

"What?" Michael looks at me as if my name wasn't Cassandra but Judas.

"Wait, let me explain," I say softly. "Whether by grand design of God or by the process of evolution, everything in the world serves some sort of purpose, or it wouldn't survive."

"Please continue, Cassandra," Mr. Abraham prompts me.

I launch into a long and boring scholarly explanation of the interconnectedness and importance of everything, ending with, "It's simple."

"Actually, it's not simple, it is symbiotic," Mr. Abraham says. "You're talking about 'symbiotic' relationships. The term means the living together of unlike organisms."

"Even faggots—I mean, maggots," Clark Rogers says from the back of the room. Clark's living proof of what I'm saying. Our student body needs an asshole, and Clark fulfills that role. I turn to see that Michael looks hurt by Clark's no doubt very deliberate slip of the tongue.

"Yes, even maggots," I say. "Maggots eat away dead tissue. They become flies. Flies are an important part of the food chain."

"To get back on point, and not to spoil your lunches, let me continue," Mr. Abraham says. "There is also the concept of coevolution. Many plants pollinated by birds or bees have very specialized flowers adapted to promote pollination by a specific pollinator that is also likewise modified. Adaptation is perhaps one of the important concepts in evolution."

"Finally, we're talking about the birds and the bees in school!" somebody cracks.

I think Scott blushes, since he's learning more about that after school than in any class. The conversation continues, but once again, I drop out. I made my point, defended my friends, and got more brownie points from Mr. Abraham. A successful, if energy draining, first hour.

As the bell rings, Mr. A reminds everyone there'll be a substitute tomorrow, and we'll be watching a DVD. What he's really saying, of course, is he's not going to be here tomorrow, and he'll be fine with it if nobody else shows. No wonder Mr. Abraham is such a popular teacher.

"Can I see you tonight?" Scott asks as he comes over to my desk. Scott's seeing more of me than he's ever seen of a girl before. He's got a serious kid-in-the-candy-store situation.

"I'm sorry," I say. "I'm sitting for Becca tonight, and I need to get ready for the reunion."

"I understand," he says, but his tone is off. Maybe he has enough thoughts of death in his head without another image. There's something so inhumane about a child with cancer.

"When can I see you?" His bright green eyes almost sparkle with anxious anticipation.

"As soon as I can, Scott," I say, then kiss him on the cheek. We get a disapproving throat clearing from Mr. A, so Scott and I make our way, hand in hand, down the hallway. Every guy is so different; yet every guy—even special ones like Scott—is so exactly alike.

"Could you come over for dinner on Easter?" he asks, almost pleading.

"I want to, but I can't. The reunion," I remind him.

"That's a lot of days for a reunion," he cracks, then smiles.

"Well, I've got a lot of family," I say, faking a smile and hoping he won't ask for any details. My family used to be larger, but a long time ago, the elders decided to limit the number of children. Now each line of the family produces one child per generation. Maybe it's like how some animals eat their young if there're too many mouths to feed; it's unnatural selection.

"Just as well," he says, sounding disappointed but not angry or upset at me. "This might be my grandmother's last Easter. I'll want to be with her, even if she doesn't know I'm there."

"She's in good hands with my grandmother at Avalon," I remind him. After much debate and another fit about how I make all the sacrifices in the family, Maggie agreed to move Scott's grandmother into her nursing home. But I know Maggie; she's not doing it out of the kindness of her heart—because there is none—but because she wants something from me.

"Thanks again," he says. We're by my locker; people pass by like background noise.

"You should see her tomorrow; everybody's skipping," I remind him. He nods.

Ever since Scott's grandmother moved into Avalon, there's been no change; she's in suspended animation. Looking at her is like watching a DVD on pause, except there's no way to hit Play, Skip, Rewind, or Fast-forward. The laws of the state, and the belief of Scott's faith, won't allow for the Eject button to be pushed and the cord pulled. She won't die, yet she can't live.

The rest of the day passes, sadly, without any drama. I've switched my lunch table to Scott and his friends', mainly other new kids, so I can avoid Cody and Bethany. I changed shifts at the hospital so I don't overlap with Kelsey. Brittney leaves me alone, probably because she's embarrassed that she never followed through with a ceremony for Robyn. Craig's mostly MIA.

After school, Scott and I make out in his car for a while. Before I leave, I use the rearview mirror to put on lipstick. Samantha would be amazed at this; she really thinks I'm a vampire. I'm thinking about her, and the idea of God's gifts. Many girls—but not Samantha—have the gift for getting guys. They know how to dress, flirt, and flaunt it. It's easy to make guys want to hook up with you, but that's not my gift. My gift is getting guys to fall in love with me. What's *not* supposed to happen is for me to fall in love with them, if this is what love feels like.

I give Scott a good-bye kiss as he lets me out a block from my house.

When I come inside, Mom and Maggie are sitting at the table. A traditional Middle Eastern meal lies before them.

"You're late, again," Mom says before I can even sit down. "Were you with *that boy?*"

"He just drove me home." I don't mention Scott's name or our in-car tongue twisting.

"What are you going to do about him?" Mom asks.

I sit down at the table and put a tiny bit of food on a plate. "It is so unfair," I say, sounding like every high school student. But I'm not whining about not getting the car or being allowed to stay out late; instead, I'm raging against my fate.

"Cassandra, this is how we live," Maggie says.

"If so, then we should really do good in the world," I say.

"What do you mean?" Mom asks.

"Both Becca and Scott's grandmother are near death. It's not fair that both have to die, when one could live," I say, expressing the thought that's haunted me the past few weeks.

The table grows very silent. All talking and chewing cease.

"Don't talk about such things," Mom says, her eyes shouting louder than her words.

"Scott's grandmother is never going to get better, but Becca could," I continue through Mom's razor-blade glare. "Scott *wants* his grandmother to die; Becca's parents *need* her to live."

"I don't want to discuss this," Mom says.

"You just don't understand," I counter. "My friends are—"

Mom cuts me off: "We have a lot to do before tomorrow, and this is family time."

"My friends are my family," I say, then swallow some food. From Mom's reaction, it is obvious I should've swallowed that last statement.

"How dare you say that!" Maggie jumps in, which doesn't surprise me. If I defy my mom, then my mom might defy hers. It could create a game of disobedience dominoes.

Before I speak, I look at Mom's and Maggie's faces, then swallow my useless words. They look tired and like they've taken one too many whips from the lash of Veronica's tongue. I sip from my water bottle, then say, "I'm sorry. There's a lot going on with me right now."

"That's better," Maggie says, acknowledging the apology. Neither she nor Mom asks about the second part of my statement. Maybe I tried deliberately to exhaust myself today, so I'd have an excuse to avoid the reunion. But I can't tell them anything: I can't talk to them about Scott; I dare not mention Siobhan. Nor can I tell Scott, Becca, or any of my friends what happens at home. For someone expert in spreading rumors, I'm drowning in secrets.

"You need to see Veronica," Mom says, almost a whisper.

"What about?" I ask aloud, but silent questions scream louder. Did they find out about my call to Siobhan? Is it something with Scott? Or something worse?

"She's waiting for you," is Mom's icy response.

"I don't have time now," I counter. "Becca's father is picking me up. I'm babysitting tonight, remember?"

Mom sighs. This is her one-millionth sigh. She should win some award.

"You should be with your family tonight," she says sharply.

"I'll be with you all weekend," I remind her, and add a sigh in return. We sound like people gasping for breath after a near drowning.

"Veronica will be very disappointed in you," Mom says. I mutter "She always is" under my breath, and then head toward my room.

I pack a few things, then wait for Mr. Berry by the curb. He's late, which is unusual, but then again, everything in his life is unusual. We small-talk on the way over, but it's hard for him to talk to me without mentioning Robyn; harder for him to talk without crying.

I knock at the door, and Mrs. Berry opens it. She's dressed up like an actress; her daily life's an act. The smile on her face looks as painted on as her lipstick. Her grief floats just below the surface, and I need energy so badly with the reunion coming up. I fight myself, but my nature still prevails, so I ask, "Mrs. Berry, at the hospital, did you get to say good-bye to Robyn?"

She grabs hold of the door and sucks in so much air I wonder how I manage to breathe.

"Not that she heard," she says, then her eyes go toward the ceiling, or maybe above.

"Were you there when . . . ?" I say, and stop, letting her fill in the words.

"She died." Her head's shaking like the memory's a fly buzzing around her head.

"I'm sorry, if you don't want to talk about it."

"Why shouldn't I talk about it?" she says, then frowns. "It's all I ever think about."

I sit in silence so still I can hear Becca tapping on the keyboard upstairs in her fantasy game while her mom retells the reality of losing one daughter, knowing she'll relive it very soon.

"They say a parent shouldn't outlive their child," Mrs. Berry says. She is licking her lips like she's thirsty for a drink. Her hands are shaking. I still them by putting my hands on top.

"But watching one of them die right before your eyes . . . ," she continues. "It's a horror you cannot imagine. I got to say good-bye, and I hoped she heard me, like she hears me now."

"I'm sure she does."

"Cassandra, you were such a good friend to Robyn," she says, a smile almost returning to her face. "She talked about how kind, thoughtful, and caring you were. All you hear are bad things about people your age. You'd think from TV that every teen is a soulless predator."

I don't respond; instead, I say, "We all miss Robyn." Her slight smile vanishes. I readjust my position, tempting her teary eyes with my shoulder when Becca yells for me.

"Hey Short Stuff!" I shout to her. She's at the top of the stairs waiting with open arms.

"She misses you," Mrs. Berry says, pulling herself together. "Thanks for doing this. We shouldn't be late." I hug her again, then run upstairs to greet Becca.

Becca and I play video games for an hour or so. She sits in front of the computer, while I lie on the floor next to her bed. In between levels on our quest, we take a moment to talk.

"Easter is Sunday. Do you want to come over?" she asks.

"I'd love to Becca, but I have a family thing to go to," I say, acting all cheerful.

"Our family is smaller this year," Becca says, then stares at the screen.

"I'm sorry, Becca," I tell her, then move closer to her. "It's okay to cry."

She looks at me, then says, "You always say that, Cass."

"And you always listen," I remind her, then she lets out a short burst of sorrow.

The tears don't last long, but they benefit us both greatly. She finds her smile, then we return to playing the game. After a while, I drop out and sneak into Robyn's room. Her clothes still hang in the closet; her pictures decorate the room. Nothing's been changed, like they're expecting her to walk in the door at any moment. I turn on the computer and I resist the urge to sneak around in Robyn's life; I've been too deceitful for too long to too many people. Sitting with Robyn's memories around me, I feel like I'm drowning. Not from feeling almost high from the sadness I've sucked in, but something new: I'm feeling sad myself.

In the other room, I hear Becca laughing, having fun. And envy overwhelms me; even in the face of death, she finds happiness, she has fun. In this life, it seems I'll never have either.

The weather this weekend is supposed to be nice, but no matter what the weatherman says, the only forecast in my future is dark skies. As I walk back to Becca's room I think how she lives under the dark cloud of cancer, while Scott suffers under the dark cloud of his grandmother's impending death. Even Samantha walks under some mysterious dark cloud of pain that I've yet to discover. My dark cloud, however, is no mystery; it even has a name. His name is Alexei.

CHAPTER 15

FRIDAY, APRIL 10

ave you seen him?"

My cousin Mara smirks, then answers, "You're safe. Nobody's seen Alexei."

"Good," I reply, and then sip from my water bottle. I'm sitting with Mara and Lillith, two of my favorite cousins, at a picnic table at the Holly Recreation Area. It's the morning of Good Friday. Most of the extended family arrived around sunrise.

"So, how are things at your new school?" I ask Lillith. Like me, like Mara, she's moved around a great deal. When we left New York, her family took over our house. They're living in Chicago now. Mara's family left New Orleans with us, but they're close, just down in Detroit. We talk more about being each other's favorites than talking with each other. We're all busy, but I suspect it's more than that. Because I'm of Veronica's line, they think I'm spoiled. They're so wrong.

"I'm meeting lots of emo boys," Lillith confesses. That's easy, as she's swallowed the Goth pill whole. Mara, with her lithe body, cute short hair, and dark, round, brown eyes, is a boy magnet. She's broken more hearts than even I have.

"There are always opportunities," Mara adds. "In every school, in every city."

"I'll tell you the best people to know," Lillith says. "It is people that dream they're going to become famous singers, actors, or writers. When they realize it won't happen, it's pretty sad."

Mara laughs, but my mind races to Samantha. What I've learned about her—some from asking, some from her MySpace page, but mostly via the rumor river—is how badly she wants to be a published writer. I even heard a rumor that a wall in Samantha's bedroom is covered with rejection letters. You'd think Samantha, with her odd appearance and obvious anguish, would gather enough rejection in high school, but some people can't get enough hurt. Lucky for me.

I'm still thinking about Samantha when Mara asks, "How's Lapeer?"

"I don't think it's like Veronica expected," I say. "I don't get why we left New Orleans."

"Because the elders know all," Mara spits out like there's a bad taste in her mouth.

"I don't think Alexei believes that," Lillith says. Alexei is the great-grandson of Simon. Simon, like Veronica, is considered the core of the family, which is why I am promised to Alexei. He's always challenged the family, but because he comes from Simon's line, it seems like Alexei can do no wrong. Like a star quarterback at high school, he is untouchable.

"I don't care what he does or doesn't do," I snap. "As long as he leaves me alone." But Mara and Lillith know that while I can usually say whatever I want, I'll do whatever my family needs. You can't deny duty. Maggie, more than Mom or Veronica, wants Alexei and me together. This type of relationship isn't looked down upon in the family, like it is by human society. Maggie says we're too far removed through the generations to be a problem. She reminds me that even the entire human race is a product of evolution and inbreeding.

"This isn't because of that boy toy Cody?" Lillith asks.

Before I can correct her, Mara adds, "Careful, Alexei might kill him."

"Not to worry. I left poor sweet Cody mostly dead," I say, then laugh.

"You heartbreaker," Lillith says, then applies some lip balm just like I applied shine to my story. This cousinly competition between the three of us regarding boys goes on forever.

"You're one to talk," I add. Like Mara and me, Lillith has no trouble capturing, keeping, and then cutting off a boy's attention. Like me, they're both swimmers and seducers.

"So if not Cody, then . . . ?" Lillith asks.

"His name is Scott," I mumble. If either of them would actually visit my MySpace or Facebook, they'd know this. All the Cody photos are gone and have been replaced by Scott pix.

"What's he like?" Mara asks.

I pause to reflect on his shyness and his strength, then say, "He's like nobody else."

"Does he have a brother?" Lillith cracks.

"No, just a dying grandmother," I say. "That's how we got together."

Mara takes a sip from her water bottle. I look at my watch, then sigh. Surprisingly, I'm missing Scott. He's supposed to fall in love with me, which he has. I'm not supposed to fall in love with him, although I'm still not sure if that is what I'm feeling. How can you know what love feels like if you've never felt it before?

"So what's he like?" Lillith asks.

"He's almost the exact opposite of every guy I've ever known," I say, then laugh. "Well, okay, like every guy, he is horny all the time, but other than that."

"Well it's a good thing we're all swimmers and know that if you want to get anywhere fast you've got to swim with, not against, the current," Mara says, summing up our mutual attitudes about most boys. "So what makes Scott so special?"

"He's not a jock," I say. "He's not crazy popular. He's just a nice guy."

"Is he hot then?" Lillith asks. Hottest boyfriend is another ongoing cousinly contest.

"No, he's just himself," I say, proudly. "There's something indescribable about him."

"That's new for you, isn't it?" Lillith asks.

I laugh, then try to describe Scott anyway. I tell stories: about how I first noticed him in class, about our first date, but mostly about how different he is than most other guys I've been with in high school. Describing Cody used to take minutes, but if Mara and Lillith don't shut me up, I could go on about Scott for hours and hours and hours. He is my new beautiful obsession.

Mara finally cuts in, "Oh goodness, Cassandra, you sound just like Siobhan before . . ."

With that name, talking stops. I try not to react. Of all my secrets, my calls to Siobhan are the deepest. As I feel more for Scott, I'll call her again. I know *why* she left; I need to know *how*.

"You can't even consider it," Mara says breaking the silence. "If Veronica—"

"It's not like that," I say as I turn my eyes and lies away from them. Surrounded by family, all I can think about is Scott and smile. Knowing that Alexei and I will come together this weekend as arranged makes me shudder. I've known for years that Alexei is nothing but evil. I know from watching him for weeks that Scott is nothing but good. I am, as always, something in between.

"Are you sure?" Lillith asks. I wonder sometimes if she wants Alexei for herself.

"We need to get ready," I say to end the conversation before I admit anything. They need to change out of their twenty-first-century fashions. Mara is a hostage to Hollister while Lillith's in all black. I'll shed my white Beatles T-shirt for the traditional costumes we use in our family rituals.

"I don't want to do this," Mara confesses. I give her a sympathetic sigh, but we all know there's no turning back from the reunion and the Good Friday Passion Play.

"Isn't that true of most things we all do in this family?" Lillith adds.

"Except Alexei," Mara says. She and Lillith share a "we know something" look.

"What do you mean?" I ask.

There's more shared silence, until Lillith says, "There are rumors about Alexei."

"What do you mean?" I ask, acting innocent even as I know his guilt fills a folder full of news stories locked in my desk.

"I hear that he's breaking the rules," Lillith says. But she doesn't sound disapproving in the least, for Lillith—despite everything evil about Alexei—wants him more than anyone.

"He can do whatever he wants," Mara says, anger filling her voice and eyes.

"Simon," I mutter.

"He's got immunity forever," Lillith says, but my skin crawls at the thought—or is it the premonition—of Alexei's touch. "You could be that way, Cassandra."

"I don't want to be like Alexei," I say, then add, "and I don't want to be with him."

"It is your duty," Lillith reminds me. "It is our history."

"You sound like Maggie," I say. Mara smiles; I don't. Nothing about Alexei or this weekend makes me smile. Only Scott makes me smile, and not the fake "I'm so happy to be with you" smile I wore like makeup with Cody, Tyler, and everyone before them.

"I'm just telling you what I've heard," Lillith answers. I wish I could give Alexei to her; I wish I could escape the obligation that awaits me. In my family, evil doesn't matter; good doesn't matter; only duty matters.

"Must there be rumors everywhere about everybody all of the time?" I snap.

"Relax," Mara says.

"I don't know about your schools, but Lapeer High is the worst ever for rumors," I say.

"Without rumor, there's no drama," Lillith says.

"And without drama, there are no tears," Mara says, toasting us with her water bottle, then sneaks a peek at her silver watch. "Look, we'd better get changed; it's almost time."

"I'm changing in Mom's car," I say. I'm an expert in back-seat dressing and undressing. As they walk off, we exchange good-byes, but my mind's weighed down channeling Siobhan, missing Scott, and dreading Alexei. I'm sure to stumble carrying such a heavy load.

I climb in Mom's Chevy Tahoe and find the bag with my other outfit. I check my watch and see there is a little while before visiting hours at the nursing home, so I call Scott.

"Hey, Scott."

"What's going on Cassandra?" he says, hissing my name.

"What's wrong?" I ask quickly.

"You and Craig, that's what's wrong," he says sharply.

"Wait, Scott, what are you talking about!"

"Kelsey told me that you were the one that broke up Robyn and Craig. She said the reason Brittney's acting so cold toward you is because you're seeing Craig. She said—"

"I need to see you and explain," I cut him off.

"What about your family reunion?" he asks snidely.

Like a dam bursting, a wave washes over me. Not of water, but images. As Scott's pained breathing fills my ears, my mind fills with faces. Faces of family, friends, but mostly Robyn. Robyn chose death; I will choose life. Human life.

"They'll understand," I lie to him. I know that they'll never understand or forgive me, but somehow that doesn't matter now. What matters is Scott. Every day is filled with so many meaningless minutes, but what I do now determines not just today, but the rest of my life.

"I need to believe you," he says.

"Who do you believe, me or Kelsey?" I ask. "Do you trust anything she says?"

"I want to trust you, Cass, I really do," he says, then sighs. "I have no choice."

"That's because you love me," I say, confident in my word choice.

He doesn't respond, just like a typical male. He'll say those words on his terms only.

He answers as I would—with a question. "So none of it is true, right?"

"Scott, you need to believe me," I say softly. "You need to show a little faith in me."

"I want to, Cassandra, I want to so badly."

"Scott, I won't hurt you," I say. I flash back to saying those same words to Cody, and to others before him. "I've made mistakes in the past, but that's behind me. This is a brand-new experience for me."

"I believe you, Cass. I believe you because I want to, and because I need to," he says. "If I don't have faith, then all I have is doubt. I can't live like that."

"So, everything is okay between us?"

"Yes," he says. "Stay at your reunion. I understand the importance of family too."

"Thanks," I say. I'm relieved I don't have to act on my choice, but Siobhan was right, knowing that I could choose love over duty shows me I can change both my fate and my nature. Scott and I make plans for Sunday night, then say our good-byes. We both end with "I love you."

I turn my phone off and lay it next to me. I open up a small bag with the costume for the reenactment and start to undress. Just as I take off my T-shirt, the door of the SUV flies open.

"Hello, cousin," Alexei whispers as his unearthly blue eyes stare right through me.

"What do you want?"

"Don't question me," he answers, then enters the car. I reach for my T-shirt, but he pulls it from me. I lean to grab the bag with my other clothes, but he jams his Jordans on the bag.

"Stop it!" I shout, then try to hide my near nakedness with my shaking hands.

"Don't be so shy, we're family," Alexei says as he moves closer to me.

I wrap my arms tighter, and try not to look at his handsome yet evil face.

"I've been looking for you," he says, almost hissing.

"Leave me alone," I say.

He laughs through his smirk. "That's not what Maggie wants. That's not what I want."

"I said—"

"And I always, *always*, get what I want."

"Then you must want to get out of the car," I snap back.

He's not moving toward the door, he's moving toward me. I glance at my watch; everybody is at the reenactment by now.

He touches my bare shoulder with his left hand in a sandpaper caress. I reach for the handle behind me, but he pulls me closer to him.

"Don't touch me!" I push his hand away, but only because he allows it. He's so much stronger than I am.

He laughs again. There's nothing I can do to him; it is all about what I can do *for* him. Once again, I'm expected to sacrifice, but nobody cares.

"You can finish undressing if you want," he says. He opens the door behind him a crack to hurl first my T-shirt, then the bag with my other clothes outside.

Before I can repeat "Leave me alone," my phone rings. The innocent sounds of the Beatles' "Love Me Do" echoes in the car. I reach to grab my phone, but Alexei gets there first. He looks at the incoming call, then asks, "Who is Scott?"

"Nobody, just another boy," I mumble.

"Sweet cousin," he says with a hiss. "You're a woman in our world. Why do you play with children?"

"I need to get that," I say.

"No, *I* need to get it," he says, then laughs as he clicks the phone. "Hello?"

I reach for the phone, but he's too quick. He opens the door and starts outside. I grab hold of his black hoodie, but he gets away. Smirking still, he almost shouts into the phone, "No, Scott, she can't come to the phone." Pause. "Why?" Pause. Laugh. "She's half undressed."

"Bastard!" I yell, but he's walking away, gathering up my clothes with his free hand.

I jump out of the car and run behind him. His words feel like lashes of a whip on my bare back. "You're confused. She didn't tell you about the man in her life?"

"Scott, don't listen!" I shout, but I doubt if he hears me. I know that when I tell him the truth, he'll never believe me now. "Damn it, Alexei!"

"Hear that, kid? She's yelling out my name," he says. "Bet she doesn't do that for you."

Every time I get close to him, he pulls away.

"Listen, boy, you don't want to mess with me," Alexei shouts into the phone. "And Cassandra, I'll fool around with her any time I want. What are you going to do about it?"

I drop to my knees.

"Huh? He hung up," Alexei says cackling at his cruelty. "Let me see, who else are you talking to these days?" As he's occupied with the phone, he drops my T-shirt on the dirty ground. I grab it. While I'm covering myself up, he's reading off the list of names, ending with, "Samantha, who is she?"

I can't answer.

"Maybe I'll give her a call," he says, then buries my phone in his front pocket.

I can't talk.

"We can do this the easy way or the hard way," he says, whispering in my ear.

I am mute, but I wish I were blind and deaf.

"You will give yourself to me or I will take what was promised. You decide, but the outcome will be the same either way," he says, then slithers away, holding my phone and my fate.

Once he's out of sight, it feels like every cell in my body dehydrates at once as I try to shed tears. I summon my strength before there's none left to save, then run back to Mom's SUV. Leaping into the car, I seek out my water bottle and then chug down the water until I almost drown.

When I can breathe normally again, I start to think of my options. I don't have car keys to drive to see Scott. I look around the parking area, and in the distance, I see a cluster of buildings. Rummaging around in Mom's car, I find a handful of change. I walk toward the buildings and there's actually a pay phone. It takes a couple of tries to get the number right, but I reach Scott's phone. He doesn't pick up, and I don't blame him. I know I can't leave him a message; I have to see him to show his faith wasn't betrayed.

I need a miracle; I call Samantha.

She picks up, but before she can speak, I say, "Samantha, it's Cass. I need your help."

There's a pause, and I think I hear faint laughter. She seems amused that I need her. She finally speaks, saying, "What do you want from me?"

"Are you at school?"

"Everybody's cutting school today," she says, sounding oddly proud for finally fitting in.

"I'm out at Holly Recreation Area," I say. "I need a ride."

"I don't know where that is," she says.

"Really?"

"Do I look like a person who goes to the beach? Who boats, swims, or fishes?" Her tone is sarcastic, but still oddly friendly. A friendly tease. "Where is it?"

"It's where Robyn died," I say, and the phone goes silent. I wait her out, then finally say, "I could show you the spot."

"No!"

"Okay, sorry," I say softly. "But I'm stranded out here. It's a long story, perfect for your book. Could you please, please come pick me up? I'll owe you."

She pauses again like there's too many words fighting to escape between her teeth. "I know you'll owe me," she finally says. "Why do you think I'm doing this?"

"I'll do whatever you want. I'll read the book you're writing," I offer.

"How about you tell me the truth instead," she says.

"What do you mean?" I ask.

Another pause, followed by a sigh, and then she says, "You know what I mean."

"Again?" I try laughing it off. "You have some imagination. No wonder you're a writer."

"Maybe," is her cryptic response.

The reenactment will end soon, and everyone will start looking for me. Unless I escape, Alexei will find me, and then things will be done the hard way. "Come get me, please," I say.

"I'll be there soon," she says.

I overhear voices in the distance. "I'll make it easy; I'll walk to the main entrance."

"It might take a while if—I mean when—I get lost," she says, trying a joke.

I laugh, then say, "Everybody's lost in this world, Samantha. You'll fit right in."

"For once," she says, then hangs up. I say my silent good-byes to my family, then start a long, lonely walk after a day filled with anger, not love.

The walk to the entrance feels like it takes forever, but finally a beat-up black Honda with death metal pouring from the windows pulls up. Samantha honks and I move like fire.

"Thanks," I say, climbing inside and sitting on the ripped-up passenger seat.

The car's filthy inside, looking like a McDonald's parking lot. Worse, it smells of smoke. When I start coughing, she says, "Sorry, the car is my mom's ashtray."

I start laughing and gagging. She rescues me by putting down the windows and music.

"Where do you need to go?" she asks as we drive away from the park.

"I need to see Scott. We had a fight."

"You're asking me to take you to see my ex-boyfriend," she says, then sighs. "Well, at least you have someone to fight with." I resist my urge to sigh or slap her. It is exactly the cage of self-loathing that bars Samantha from love and happiness, yet it is also what draws me to her.

"So what were you fighting about?" she asks.

"Nothing," I mumble. Then with forced enthusiasm ask, "So, were you working on your book?

"How did you know?" she asks, trying not to smile. As we drive farther away from the park, Samantha dives deeper into the details of her story. I pretend interest. It's not that there's anything wrong with the story, but it is like Samantha herself: one cliché on top of another. Like the layers of dark clothes she wears, these clichés hide the real person buried under the poses and pretensions.

"What do you think?" she asks.

"You've got a vivid imagination," I reply.

"So are you saying vampires are imaginary?" she asks.

"You believe they're real and that's what matters," is my misdirecting answer.

"You wouldn't know anything about that, would you?" she asks.

"Not this again," I say, trying to laugh it off. "You still think I'm a vampire?"

"I know you're something," she says, not laughing at all.

"I am trying to be something. I'm trying to be your friend," I say.

She pauses, unsure how to respond. "Well, where is Scott?"

"I don't know yet, can I borrow your phone?" I ask.

"Well, you've taken my boyfriend, and you're using my car, so . . . ," she says, then flips the phone my way. As I expected, Scott's numbers are still in her phone, but it's useless. He's not picking up. I make one more call, reaching the nursing home. "Avalon Care," the voice says.

"This is Cassandra Gray. Is my grandmother there?" I ask, knowing that she's miles behind me and probably looking for me with the rest of my family.

"No, Cass, she's not," the woman says. I want to ask more, but I can't think of the woman's name. "She's not on the schedule today. Do you want me to leave a message?"

"That's okay, no message," I say, then add in a very small voice, "Can I ask a favor?"

"Sure, Cass," the still nameless woman replies.

"I know you're not supposed to tell me, but I can't get ahold of my friend Scott," I say. "I just need to know if he's there visiting his grandmother, Lenore Parker."

"Cass, you know the rules about confidentiality."

"Please, one time," I say, trying to sound like a desperate child. "I won't tell my grandmother. You won't tell her. I won't tell Scott. Nobody gets hurt, so what's the harm?"

There's a pause as she either sorts through my logic or searches for Scott. A few moments later, she returns to the phone. "Mrs. Parker has a young male visitor, okay?"

"Okay," I say. "Thank you, thank you."

"Have a blessed day," the woman says, and I finally recognize the voice.

"Thank you, Mrs. Johnson," I say, her blessed expression clicking the connection. I give Samantha back her phone, although I hope she doesn't use it. I've noticed she's a terrible driver even while paying attention to the road; I can't imagine her driving while distracted.

"Who was that?" Samantha asks.

"I know where Scott is. He's with his grandmother at the nursing home."

"How sad," Samantha says. "I know his grandmother means a lot to him."

"Are your grandparents still living?" I ask, searching for more clues.

"No," she says, quickly, defensively, instinctively. I don't respond. She reaches to change the music but instead says, "I don't know. My mom, well, she doesn't really . . ."

Samantha stops in midrevelation. I remain silent, hoping she will continue, but she's not biting.

"Where is this place?" she finally asks.

I give her directions, then probe about her grandparents and her mother, but Samantha's not speaking. We're rounding a big turn on the south side of the lake when I say, "Pull over for a second."

She brings the car to stop on the side of the road. "This is it," I say. "Where Robyn—"

She cuts me off, "I told you, I didn't want to see this!"

"You need to see it, Samantha," I say firmly.

She turns the music up; I turn it down. She rolls down the window; I turn up the heat.

"I know you weren't close to Robyn, but you still need to express your grief," I say.

She stares me down, then says. "Cassandra, I don't cry in front of people, so give it up."

I grab Samantha's hand as she starts to put the car in drive. "It's okay. I'm your friend."

She pulls her hands away and stares harder. Death metal fills the car; the spot on the road where Robyn died fades into the distance, but she doesn't crack. Samantha's emotional calluses are too thick even for me. We drive the rest in the way in loud silence thinking about all the things we probably want to say. She wants to talk; I want to listen. It's just a matter of timing.

She drops me at Avalon Convalescence Care, then speeds away. The staff at the nursing home lets me pass and I move as quickly as if I were swimming for the Olympic gold. I see Scott standing at his grandmother's bed. The glare he gives me holds all his hurt in two eyes.

"What do you want?" he says. Before I can answer, he adds, "I want you to leave."

"No," I say, then walk toward him. "That was my cousin Alexei. He's insane."

"Just leave us alone," he says angrily, almost shouting over the beeping and gurgling machines.

"It's true," I tell him, feeling desperate for the first time ever. "Please believe me."

"I can't take any more of this," Scott says. I can tell by the look in his eyes that "this" refers to *pain*, but he knows that even the word "pain" falls short of describing the hurt within.

"I would never do anything to hurt you," I say, praying that I can make the words true.

"I don't need to hear it," he says.

"Listen to what I just said. I would never do anything to hurt you." To my shock, a tear begins to roll down my cheek. "Let me explain—"

Scott is just as surprised by my tear as I am. He cuts me off, saying, "No, Cass, you don't need to explain. I guess I believe you."

"Alexei is evil. He is—"

Scott cuts me off again as he wipes away the tear. "I said I believe you. You know why?"

"No," I say.

"Because I have to. I believe *in* you," he whispers. "Because I love you, Cass."

Scott softly touches my hand, unaware that inside me a battle rages. Every ounce of who I want to become pushes against every pound of who I have been. I desperately want to fight my nature and change my fate, but it feels like I'm struggling to change the rotation of the earth itself.

"I have to tell you something," I say as my eyes focus on the floor to hide my confusion and pain. "I don't know if I'm strong enough to fight my family so we can stay together."

I owe him the truth, so I say, "You're what I want, but obeying my family is part of who I am."

"That's why I love you, Cass," he says.

"What do you mean?"

"You are who you are," he says. "You're not like Samantha, Cody, or even Robyn trying to be something they're not. You're real. You care about people other than yourself."

I just stare back at him, hoping my eyes will reveal what my heart is starting to feel, because there's no way I can open my mouth and tell him the truth, my truth. I'm real. I am my nature. And I am not human. "Scott, you're wrong about me. Maybe we should just end this."

"I won't let you do that. I know you want this." Like his grandmother next to us fighting against death, Scott fights for me with the same courage, faith, and strength. "And I want you."

"What I do is break boys' hearts, you knew that about me," I remind him.

"You broke up with all of those other boys because you weren't ready," he says.

"Ready for what?"

"To find me."

As if I'm struck deaf, the world goes silent at his words. If the machines were hooked up to me instead of his grandmother, the flatline of emotion that runs through me would spike. Ever since I met Scott, my heart's been on a journey to become human, filled with not just blood, but with emotion. And now I've come to a threshold. As with Siobhan before me, love can end my familiar life and allow me to start a new one.

"I will do anything to stay with you, Cass," he whispers. "Will you do the same for me?"

"If I can do it, I will," I say, as my eyes flood with tears. I reach out and he opens his arms to receive me.

As he holds me close, he says, "Other than you, there's only one thing I want."

He turns us so we're staring at his grandmother. I expect a kiss, but instead, under the din of beeping machines, he whispers, "What I want more than anything is something you can't do."

"What is that?"

He's not looking at me; he's looking at his grandmother before us. Or rather the woman who used to be his grandmother. She's not a monster, but she's not really herself anymore, and Scott knows it. He fights through tears, then says, "All I want is her suffering to end and for her to die in peace."

"Are you asking me to—?"

"No, of course not," Scott says. "Just pray with me that she finds peace."

Again, I go silent. I look at his grandmother, so near death.

I think of Robyn wanting to trade lives with Becca. And I think about myself, not a human but wanting desperately to become one. Finally, I think of Veronica and the powers possessed by the family elder. The power to transfer energy. The power to restore life—but only by causing a death.

CHAPTER 16

SATURDAY, APRIL 11

*S*amantha, you awake?"

Her bedroom is very dark; the only light is from the red letters on the unset alarm clock telling me it's just a few minutes before midnight, the start of Easter morning.

"Wide," Samantha answers.

"What a tough few days," I say, then sigh. After leaving the nursing home, I spent Friday night at Scott's house. While his mom reluctantly agreed to let me stay, she locked me in a guest room—much to his dismay. In the middle of the night, Scott knocked gently, but I turned him away. I couldn't risk his mom catching us, kicking me out, or cutting me off from Scott if she found us together. Even still, I must have upset his mother terribly. Because after I left his house this morning, it was as if Scott disappeared. No one answered the phone at his house, he didn't pick up his cell, and Mrs. Johnson told me (once you get someone to bend a rule, breaking it is easy) that he didn't visit his grandmother other than briefly on Saturday morning.

To my family, it's also as if I've disappeared, and I'm sure my mom is just as upset. Without my cell, they couldn't find me. I left a message on the machine at home letting her know I was safe, but that I wasn't ready to come home yet. I need some calm before facing that storm. So once again, I turn to Samantha to bail me out.

She picked me up after my hospital shift today, then we spent the night watching scary movies. I spent Friday afternoon with evil no longer lurking in the shadows, but instead actually touching my skin in the form of Alexei. My movie monster is too real.

"Well, tonight was fun," Samantha says and I'm at a loss for words. That word—"fun"—like so many other words, has never been part of my vocabulary. It's just a word, not a feeling.

"Better than yesterday," I say.

"I guess," she says. Samantha doesn't realize I'm a better writer than she'll ever be, with the story I made up to explain why she needed to rescue me Friday afternoon. The fabrication involved my family being cruel to me; I sensed it was the kind of story that she'd believe.

"Thanks for letting me stay over," I say. "Sorry to keep you up so late talking."

"It's okay, I'm used to being up late," she says. "Why do you think I'm always almost asleep in school?"

"I just thought you were like me," I offer.

"What do you mean?" she asks.

"Just bored to death by it all," I say.

"Well, a lot of it is pretty boring," she says.

"Well, not like Bio," I say. "Like a few weeks ago with you and Scott going at it, that wasn't boring at all."

"I kinda lost it," she says. "That's not like me."

"What happened?"

"I'm just really antireligion. Maybe that's yet another reason Scott and I didn't last, since he's so religious," she says. "You believe in God, right?"

"I believe in Jesus," is my hairsplitting answer.

"I don't, and it's not because of science or anything," she says. "Or the absurdity of an invisible wish-granting giant in the sky. There's just too much hate and hurt in the world."

"Maybe it serves a purpose," I say, very carefully. I never got close to conversations like this with Robyn, old boyfriends, or other friends. But something about this night, something about this girl, seems different. Maybe it's coming in contact with Alexei that has me feeling closer to her, closer to just *feeling*. Alexei used my cell phone to call Samantha several times today looking for me, but she's lied for me, like a true friend would.

I yawn, then say, "Sorry, I guess I'm just tired. We should sleep. I'll need to go to Mass tomorrow, then work."

"I can't sleep most nights," she says. "You know why?"

"Why?"

"I just lie awake thinking of all the stupid things I've done and I've said," she says. "No wonder people equate sleep with death." I flash to Scott's grandmother. A coma is not sleep; it is not death. Scott's grandmother is just like me; another creature caught in between.

"What do you mean?"

"Well, they say when you die, your whole life passes before your eyes," she says. "That's me when I try to sleep. My whole miserable rotten life passes before me."

"Don't talk that way," I say, correcting and comforting, if from a distance.

"It is who I am," she says.

"Samantha, I don't think you know who you are," I say, not to insult but to bait. "You're not Goth, you're not emo. You should just be yourself."

She's doesn't respond as I tell her all about her life. I rise from the floor, where I've been comfortably numb on a sleeping bag. I walk through the darkness toward Samantha's bed, then lean in as I ask, "Who are you, Samantha? You can tell me. I won't tell anyone *anything*."

"Anything?" In just one word, she sounds confused, nervous, scared, but mostly excited.

"Who are you, Samantha?" I ask, then sit on her tiny bed. She is lying perfectly still. For seconds, then minutes, the air is still as all noise vanishes into a vacuum of silence.

"Do you really want to know?" she whispers. "Can I really trust you?"

"Yes," I say. "I know you have something you want to say. Don't keep it in. Your uncried tears, your secrets, all of it are just poison. Let it out, and you'll feel better forever."

"You want to know about me?" she says, and I'm trying not to salivate as I hear the shaking presobbing sounds choking in her throat.

"Yes, tell me everything," I whisper. "Whatever pain you bear, let me lift it from you."

She pulls her two black T-shirts over her head, then brushes her hair away from her back—her cut and scarred back. These are not surface cuts, like the crosses on her arms. The scars are deep, and there must be over a hundred. Their location shows these are also not self-inflicted.

"This is me," she says, her back still to me. "I'm a scarred freak."

"Samantha." I say her name because there's nothing else to say.

"So, what's a few crosses on my arms compared to this cross I bear," she whispers, yet it is like she's shouting in defiance, I'm just not sure of what or whom. "This is me."

"What happened?" I ask as she puts her shirt back on, then turns to face me. She's backed herself into the corner of the bed; I've moved to the edge.

"I was four," she starts. "My mom . . ."

"Go on," I say. "You can trust me."

Her piercing eyes challenge my statement, so I repeat myself. "You can trust me."

"I'll tell you this," she says slowly. "But you have to tell me something."

"What?" I ask, but she just stares back at me. I think about what I can reveal and what I can't. I try to imagine what Samantha believes, but mostly I focus on all the hurt she's hoarding.

"A secret as dark as this one," is her eerie response. She takes a deep breath, then continues. "We were living in Flint, north end. I don't remember much of it."

"Close your eyes," I whisper, then reach to turn off the lights.

"I was four. Mark, one of my mom's druggie boyfriends, was over. Maybe he was watching me. I don't know. There were always people coming and going. I remember I was crying. I was crying about something because when you're four that's what you do, you know?"

I don't respond. I don't want to lie to Samantha as she starts to reveal her truth.

"So, the druggie Mark got mad at me for crying. Yelled, screamed, hit me, all that. But I wouldn't, I couldn't, stop. The more he told me to stop crying, the more I bawled. So, he . . ."

I stay silent.

"He threw me through a window," Samantha finally says. I inch closer; I don't sense tears yet, only sweat and fear. Her heart's beating as fast as a hummingbird's wings.

"And he left me there," she says, then sighs. "He left me bleeding on the ground, lying in a pool of jagged glass cutting up my body. He didn't call for help. He just walked away."

"Samantha, I didn't know," I whisper.

"Nobody does," she says. "My mom got one of her dealer doctors to write some bullshit excuse about a heart murmur so I'd never have to take gym, so nobody—until you tonight— ever saw it."

"Not even Scott?"

"No," she says. I want to know more about that "no," but I let it pass. For now.

"Now do you understand me why I cut myself, why I never cry, and why I'm a freak?"

I push closer, one inch at a time. "You're not a freak."

"Yes, I am, just like you are," she says. "So we can be friends now. Freak friends."

"Yes, we can be friends, but more importantly, your healing can begin," I say.

"What are you talking about?"

"You can't heal scars until you admit they are there," I whisper. "It's hard what you've just done, but it is harder to keep it inside. It's a scary thing to tell someone your secrets."

"It doesn't work like that, it's not like flipping a switch," she says, then flips on the light. I look into her eyes filled with pain, but still without a single teardrop. "What scares *you*, Cass?"

"*You* are scaring me a little right now," I tell her, then laugh. She doesn't laugh back.

"No, I'm not. Cassandra, I don't think you're afraid of anything," she says, accusingly.

"You are so wrong," I tell her the bold truth. The difference between my fear and hers is that my fear has a name—Alexei. Her fears may be behind her; my fate and fear still await me.

"You don't cry either, but you're always around when people do. Why is that?" she asks. "You break up with guys but move quickly on to the next. It's like you don't feel like the rest of us."

"You're talking crazy again," I say, moving off the bed, but she grabs my hand.

"No, I'm talking truth," she says. "You can deny what you are, but you can't hide it."

I look over at her bookcase, then grab a random book off the shelf. It is, of course, a vampire novel. I point it at her, and say, "You've read too many of these."

She takes the book from my hand, as if it were a precious gift. "I don't think so."

"They're all the same," I say, then sit back on the bed. "Will your book be different?"

"What do you mean?" she asks.

"Why must every vampire lurk in the darkness hunting for human blood? Why must they all be dark and mysterious?" I ask.

"Because that's what a vampire story is about," she says.

"It doesn't need to be," I counter. "Why not make your book different?"

"What do you mean?" Her eyes are darting the room, I suspect looking for her notebook.

"Maybe your vampire could be sympathetic," I say. "Maybe he could be born into a family of vampires. Maybe he doesn't want to be one, but doesn't know how not to be. Maybe your vampire could be tired of only surviving and sacrificing. Maybe your vampire wants to be normal and live among humans instead of feeding off them."

"Go on," she says, but I can't. I've shown her my secret scars except she doesn't know it.

"Never mind," I say, then I turn my back to her like I wish I could turn back time. For Samantha I really do feel empathy; I understand too well how hard it is to hold back a secret.

"Are you going to tell Scott?" she asks after an awkward silence.

"Your secrets are safe with me," I say.

"You still owe me a secret," she says.

"How do I know I can trust you?" I ask.

"I'm the only person at Lapeer you can trust," she says.

"Why's that?"

"Because I don't have anybody to talk to," she says. I want to tell her that every time she says something like that it's just rubbing more salt in those wounds. But I can't because I still need those salty tears her self-hatred produces. "No, that's not it. It's because I've proven it."

"What do you mean?"

"I learned a long time ago that most things are better left unsaid. Secrets are meant to be kept, not shared. Keeping a secret hidden, that is what locks in a friendship. You say you want to be friends, but how can I be friends with you since I can't trust you?" she asks.

"I do want to be *friends* with you," I say. I doubt that Samantha is bi, like her profile says. My guess is she's not looking for sex; she's looking for softness in her hard life.

"I already know a secret about you, but I've never shared it with anyone," she says.

"What is it?"

"Can I ask you something first?" she says, and I nod. Conversations with Samantha are fits of stops and starts. "Who do you think started those rumors about Craig and Brittney?"

"I'm not sure," I say. "Do you know?"

"I think it was Brittney herself," she whispers, and I lean closer.

"Are you sure?" I ask, because that is what I've always suspected.

"Positive," she says, sounding proud.

"How do you know for sure?" I ask. There is no way Brittney speaks to Samantha.

"I've watched girls like her all my life," Samantha says. "You're too close to them, too friendly, but on the outside looking in it's easy to see exactly what they are."

"And what is that?"

"People who don't care about anyone but themselves," she says. "Do I know for sure? No. Do I have a signed confession? Again, no. But am I positive? One hundred percent."

"Why would she do that?"

"You mean other than steal Craig away and become the center of attention?" she asks, and I nod. "Maybe also to create some drama."

"Maybe," I mutter.

"You understand, right?" she asks. "Isn't that why you chopped down the Goth tree?"

"What do you mean?" I mumble.

"Are you denying it?" she asks.

"No," I say, then move off the bed and back to the floor. "But how did you find out?"

"This is my secret about you," she says, a little angry and excited. "I'll ask the questions."

"Okay, what do you want to know?"

"I understand what Brittney got out of her actions, although she must regret it now," Samantha continues. "But riddle me this, Cassandra. What did you get out of yours?"

"I was just stirring up a little excitement," I confess.

"And why did you need to create more drama?" she asks, assuming my Grand Inquisitor mode. "Don't you think Lapeer High School has enough of that already?"

"Maybe," is all I can say.

Samantha turns off the light, then says, "Now we have mutually assured destruction."

"What do you mean?"

"In history, we studied the Cold War. The reason we never nuked the Russians and they never nuked us is we both knew that if one made the first move, the other would destroy the world. So now, Cassandra, we each have our nukes and secrets pointed at each other. Because we know secrets about each other, we can destroy each other. And so we can be at peace."

"Always give peace a chance." I'm hiding a sigh of relief that my real secret remains safe.

"Oh, we're also at peace because we're both freaks," she says, then laughs. I sigh.

"You're not a freak and neither am I," I remind her as I pull the covers over myself. She tries to keep talking, but I just pretend to sleep.

I stay silent. I've said too much, and yet I've said far less than I want to. I glance through the darkness at Samantha, then turn to look at the shelves packed with vampire novels. One day she'll learn the truth about vampires; one day, she'll learn there are creatures who feed off humans in plain sight. One day, she'll learn more about me, but not yet. Not yet.

CHAPTER 17

SUNDAY, APRIL 12

Why won't you listen to me?"

My immature-sounding question goes unanswered. It is Easter Sunday evening, and my family is furious at me for my vanishing act. After leaving Samantha's this morning, I went to church, then to the hospital. I did two shifts at the hospital, then visited Becca and her family. I wanted to finalize plans with Scott, but he's impossible to reach. His vanishing is more complete than my own. By late in the evening, my choice was to become homeless or face the lash at home.

"Cassandra Veronica Gray!" Maggie answers. I'd started to explain my actions, but they're not listening. "You embarrassed this entire family. You've ruined everything!"

"Where were you?" Mom asks. They're at the kitchen table looking like hanging judges.

"If you would just let me explain," I say, then sit at the table with them.

"I don't know if there's anything you could say that—," Maggie continues.

Veronica stops her. "It wasn't easy for you either. Maybe she needs more time."

Mom glares at both ends of the generation sandwich, takes a sip from her bottled water, then sits back in her chair.

"I'm not ready," I start. Maggie looks at me with all the anger of the ages. I tell them where I spent the weekend rather than why I left the reunion until Mom pushes me for details.

"That's enough stalling," Maggie says. "I want to know about Alexei."

"Nothing happened," I mumble.

"Don't lie to us," Mom says.

"What do you mean?" I reply.

The three women around the table look at each other, then back at me, until Maggie speaks. "Cassandra, dear, don't be embarrassed. We are your family, you can tell us anything."

I'm staring at her; she's looking straight through me. "I don't have anything to tell you."

All three look confused and fall silent, then Mom says, "So you have not been with Alexei since Friday afternoon?"

"No, I told you that," I say. "I told you where I was. You didn't believe me?"

"I didn't want to believe you," Maggie says in a voice part ice, part fire.

"The traditions in this family are very old, and Cassandra is young, so—," Veronica starts.

"She has a duty," Maggie says, cutting her off; her eyes flash with anger. "A duty to this family."

"Alexei is evil," I say. "Do you know what's he's been doing? He's torturing children."

"That's not true!" Maggie shouts back.

I stare at her, then say, "It's a fact, and if you want me to show you the proof, I have news articles—"

"Stop it!" Maggie says. "It doesn't matter what he's done. It matters what you need to do."

"I won't do it!" I shout back.

"If this is because of one of your immature infatuations with a boy, then—" Mom starts.

"It is not that," I say, cutting her off. I don't tell her that "infatuation" isn't the word I'd choose.

"Cassandra, this is our way," Maggie says, but stares at Veronica with a level of anger I've never seen before. "It's time for the next generation. It is your duty to mate with Alexei and—"

"Mate! I'm not some animal!" I shout, but bury the words I really want to say: *I'm not like the rest of you anymore. I'm done living in between.*

"Your duty is to your family, not yourself," Maggie says to me, but she's still looking at Veronica. There's something going on between them that I can't begin to understand.

"If you have not been with Alexei, then where is he?" Mom asks, but I don't answer.

"No one has seen Alexei since Friday afternoon," Maggie says.

"Everyone is looking for him," Mom says.

"I don't know anything," I say.

"Did he call you?" Maggie asks.

I shrug. "I don't know. I lost my phone."

"I know," Mom says. "Lillith found it at the park. Now you see why I don't trust you with a car, dear."

I let that remark go. She doesn't trust me, not because she thinks I would have a car accident. Instead, she fears that I would drive away, never to return. That fear became even more real to everyone in the family since Siobhan showed us that there was a way out.

I get up from the table and start toward my room. The instant I plug in my phone, the message signal comes up. Starting around two o'clock on Saturday afternoon and lasting until just an hour ago are regular messages from Scott's mom, mixed in with a few from Samantha, Becca, and frantic calls from Mom and Maggie. Scott's mom's messages start out calm, but by Saturday night they escalate to thunderstorm status. In this evening's messages, his mother is in tears, no longer angry with me, but worried about her missing son. The final message is simple. "Cassandra, I'm calling the police."

No sooner do I hear the last message than my phone

rings. The innocent sounds of "Love Me Do" by the Beatles seem odd after listening to Scott's mom's accusing messages.

"Scott, where are you?" I ask, but there's nothing but endless silence on the other end.

"What's going on?" More silence.

"This isn't funny." More silence.

"I'm going to hang up unless you tell me what's going on." I hear deep breathing.

"Scott, are you okay?"

"No, he's not," is Alexei's unnerving answer.

I pause for a second that seems closer to forever.

"Alexei, where is Scott?"

"He is where *you* should be," Alexei hisses. "Right next to me."

"Let me talk to him!"

After he's done laughing, Alexei says, "He can't speak right now."

"Let him go!"

"He's got a lot of sadness in him," he says. "But not much fear. Fear's the best because it produces the strongest emotion and most powerful tears. That's why the males in our family will always dominate. We're willing to capture and, if needed, create tears using terror and fear."

"Let him go!" I repeat.

"Not yet."

"I want to see him," I say. I move over to my desk and unlock it.

"Good, because I want to see you."

"Let him go, or else," I say out of pure animal instinct to protect things that matter.

"Or else what?"

I pull out the folder of news alerts. "I'll call the police."

"The police?" he asks, then laughs.

"It was you. In Midland, and before that in Bay City. I've been tracking you."

"I don't know what you are talking about."

I open the folder and start reading the articles. Rather than cutting me off, I sense Alexei almost enjoys the listing of his crimes, since shame and guilt are just more human emotions he cannot feel. I end by saying, "How did you become this way?"

"What way?"

"Evil," I say, and hiss.

There's silence on the line. "You should join me," Alexei finally says.

"What do you mean?"

"I'm not evil, I'm frustrated," he confesses. "I'm tired of waiting."

"Waiting?"

"Waiting for you to be with me. Waiting for father, grandfather, and Simon to die," he says. "I want to be in charge of my family; I'm tired of taking orders. Aren't you tired of it?"

I say nothing, since I cannot agree with Alexei. I cannot admit any similarity.

"What you call evil, I call necessity," he says. "Evil is the existence we're forced to live. Evil is not being able to feel love. If I can't feel love, then all that leaves is hate. All that leaves is evil. You know what I'm talking about. Join me, Cassandra, it is your turn too," he says.

"But," I start, then I think not of myself or my family but of Scott. And then I know that I'm not like Alexei; I'm not evil—because I do feel love. "Enough! Let Scott go or I'll call the police and—"

"No you won't!"

"Why not?"

"Because unlike me, you won't break our rules," he says. "You won't reveal us."

"I broke the family rules on Friday when I left you with nothing," I remind him.

"That's going to change too."

"What do you mean?"

"I'll let Scott go in exchange," he says.

"For what?" I ask, but I know.

"For you." I feel his smirk snake through the phone and wrap like a cobra around my neck.

"This is wrong!" I say, but there is no wrong or right, just the power of his will.

"You won't betray family. You will do as you're told. And you won't turn me in," he says.

"I'll tell Simon you're the one breaking the rules," I counter.

"I didn't break any rules," he lies.

"Yes, you did, Alexei. Yes, you did. We *feed* off human suffering, we don't cause it."

"We see the rules differently, you and I," he says.

"We'll see what Simon and Veronica say when I tell them what—"

He cuts me off. "Simon's useless. Veronica's time is up, and everybody knows it."

"I won't do it," I finally say.

"Yes, you will, Cassandra," he says. "Because if you don't, then Scott will—"

I cut him off: "I don't care about Scott."

"But you do, Cassandra. You do and I know it," he says.

"Scott's just another boy," I say tossing more lies on the fire. "There will be others."

Again, Alexei tortures me with his laughter, as he's probably tortured Scott with deeds. "I figured out what's wrong with you. I know why you ran away from me on Friday," he says.

"Oh really? Why?"

"Because you've changed," he says.

"What do you mean?"

"You're becoming human."

I don't deny it. If I'm human, then I can feel love. Humans

will make any sacrifice for love, Siobhan said. This is my test. "You win. I'll do whatever you want to protect Scott."

He laughs at my weakness, then tells me where he's waiting back in the park. He assures me that Scott isn't hurt physically. I don't believe him, but I know there's little I can do. If I'm to rescue Scott, I'll need to tangle with Alexei. I'll need strength. I'll need Samantha.

"Samantha, I need your help again!"

Samantha answers with a yawn, like I woke her. "Why should I keep helping you?"

"Please," is my nonanswer. I'm so used to giving help; I don't know how to ask for it.

"No, Cassandra, I'm not helping you again," she says. "I'm hanging up."

"Tell me why?"

"Why what?"

"Why you won't help me?"

"I'm hanging up," she repeats.

"I know why, and I understand," I say. "Because I'm using you, and I'm sorry for it."

"You finally admit it. How brave," she says with supreme sarcasm.

"It is not what you think," I say. I know I'm in too deep. I'll figure how to get myself out of this hole later, but I need her help now. "I'm not using you for just rides."

"I don't have anything else to offer anyone," she mumbles, but her words shout that she was right the other night. It's not like flipping a switch; change and healing both take time.

"Yes, yes you do," I say almost in a whisper.

"What are you taking about?"

"You have all this pain in your life that you don't know how to handle," I say.

"You're just like Brittney. You want to be around other girls who have less so you can feel better about yourself," she says. "I thought you were more mature than that."

"That's not it either."

"Then I guess I'm too stupid to understand," she says.

"You want to know the truth about me?" I ask. "You have your suspicions, right?"

"Yes." But in those three letters, I detect a wave of emotions sweeping over her.

"Give me a ride and come with me," I say, then take a deep breath, as if I'm planning on being underwater for forty days and nights. "Then I'll reveal my true nature to you."

There's a pause, a sniffle, but no answer.

"Samantha, if you help me, I'll trust you with a secret *you can never share*."

Another pause, another sniffle, and then an answer. "I'll be right over."

"Is this about Robyn?" Samantha says as we pull back into the Holly Rec area.

"Not really," I say. The ride's been all death metal, not life secrets. "It's about Scott."

"Scott?" she asks, then turns the music down.

"Why do you think I want to hear this?" she says. "He dumped me."

"Do you know why?"

"Because everybody rejects me," Samantha answers.

"No, because you feel that way about yourself and because you say things like that."

"It's who I am," she says, reaching to turn the music back up, but I touch her hand.

"No, it's not," I say. "Like I said the other night, you don't know who you are."

"Don't give me your counseling bullshit," she says. "I've been to enough real therapists."

"And what do they tell you?" I ask as I let go of her hand.

"What do you care?" she replies. "What makes you think you're so smart?"

"Don't turn it back on me—that's my trick," I say. "What do they tell you?"

"A bunch of bullshit," is Samantha's nonreply.

"Fine, then you tell me," I say. "Pull over, talk to me, and open up."

"Why should I do that?"

"Because it's the human thing to do," I say. "And you're human. You're not a vampire. You're a very special human being with a lot to offer, who for some reason doesn't know that."

"Fine, fuck you!" She pulls the car over. The car stops, and time seems to as well.

"So what do you want?" she asks. "The short story about how my mom's a drugged-out loser? You wanna hear more about the druggie boyfriend who pushed me through that window? Or the other boyfriends who did worse? Maybe you want the long story about trying to fit in only to get smacked in the face and kicked to the curb. Is that what you want to know?"

"You can't keep holding it in. Tears you don't cry will rot your very soul," I say.

"No, I won't let people see that side of me," she says. "I taught myself not to cry."

"But that is part of who you are," I say. "Just be yourself."

"I hate myself," she says, then rolls up her sleeves to show the pattern of crosses.

"No, you hate and are afraid of who you've become."

"I'm scared of people judging me and rejecting me, which used to happen all the time," she says. "I was the kid without a dad and with the stoned mom. The poor kid. The freak."

"You're not a freak!" I shout. "If you can feel like this, trust me, you're not a freak."

"It doesn't matter what anyone else thinks; this is how I feel!" she screams.

"That's hard, Samantha, so hard." I can tell her tears are rising to the surface. "Go on."

"Scott, I guess he understood me in some ways, maybe too much," she says, her voice softer now, less angry. "I don't blame him. He deserves you, he deserves to be happy."

"So you still care for him," I say. The car is in park; my desperation is in overdrive.

"Of course I do," she says. "He's the first person I ever felt any connection with."

"Would you help him if he needed it?" I ask, mostly sure of her answer.

She pauses, collects herself, then says, "Of course I would; I'm not a monster."

"And neither am I," I say, then move closer to Samantha. "You believe that?"

"Maybe," she says, unsure of my intentions and moving back very slowly.

I put my hand on her face. "I'm not a monster, Samantha, but you were right."

"About what?"

I whisper in her ear, "I'm not human either."

"What do you mean?" Her voice is a mix of shock, wonder, and fear.

"I need something from you." I move closer, almost touching her face.

"I was right. You *are* a vampire!" she says as she pulls at the neckline of her shirt.

I put my face almost next to hers. "I don't want your blood."

"No?" she says, letting me come closer. We're almost eye to eye. "What do you want?"

"I don't want your blood, Samantha," I repeat, then whisper, "I need your tears."

Samantha backs away, unsure of what to say, do, or feel.

"You say you hurt, I need you to show me." I'm still whispering.

"I don't understand," she says, sounding very afraid.

I move closer to her. "I don't have time to explain now. Scott needs your help. This is what you can do to help him, please."

"I can't," she says.

"I know you cry, but you won't do it in front of others. I know you hurt," I say as I reach into my back pocket. I pull out my monogrammed handkerchief and a folded-up piece of paper.

"What's that?" she asks.

"It's your poem, the one called 'I Hurt, Hurt, Hurt.' Do you remember it?" She nods as if her head weighs six hundred pounds. I unfold the poem and hand it to her.

"I don't understand," she says, taking the paper from me.

"Do you remember when you wrote this?" Another nod.

"Do you remember why you wrote it? Samantha, can you feel that way again?"

"I feel this way *all the time*," she says. "I hurt all the time."

"Read it," I whisper. "Read it and don't hold anything back."

She looks at me in bewilderment, but starts to read. I let her head rest on my shoulder.

I hurt, hurt, hurt
And I don't know why.
Everything in me wants to cry.
My eyes have dried up
There are no tears
So my whole body cringes in fear.
I wait for the day when everything will be all right
When my heart and brain aren't always in a fight.

I hurt, hurt, hurt
And I don't know why.
It's tearing me apart, it burns me alive.
How am I still here, what is my drive?
Why do I sit and last through the pain?
It feels like daggers coming in rain.
Down on my face, into my heart
Tearing me, tearing me, tearing me apart.

I'm sick of the hurt and the pain and the rain.
I'm sick of feeling totally insane.

I hurt, hurt, hurt
And I don't know why.
All I know is I need to cry or die.
I'll push back the pain most days
And try not to kill my little sun rays.
But even in crowds, I suffer alone
Even though I feel as chewed as a bone.
I look up for answers, but see nothing but stars.
I stare into the mirror, but see nothing but scars.
I'm a fatherless child, all hope buried in the dirt.
And so
I hurt, hurt, hurt.

"Show me, Samantha, show me that you really hurt," I whisper.

Samantha looks up at me, then she shows her tears are not all dried up as they flow to me as effortlessly as a river flows to the ocean. I let the tears soak into my shoulder and the cycle is complete. She feels better because she's cried, and so do I. "Now we need to go help Scott," I say.

"I don't understand," she says.

"It's too complicated to explain it all to you," I say softly. "We need to save him."

"No, I need to know," she says as she grabs onto my wrist.

"It is through crying that humans release the unique emotional energy stored inside them. It is through collecting those tears and transferring that energy that my kind survives. If people didn't cry, they wouldn't be human beings. If we didn't collect those tears, we couldn't survive and maintain our human form. Humanity has adapted to us, and we to them," I explain.

"Coevolution, like we talked about in class that day," Samantha says. It is as if I can see the connections clicking in her head. "So, you're really not human? What are you then?"

"We have to go now!" I shout.

She gives up asking questions when I refuse to answer. So we just travel in silence toward the meeting place with Alexei. No matter what rules Alexei has broken, what I've just done is much worse.

"Scott, are you hurt?" I ask as I open the door to the black Ford van.

"He can't talk right now," Alexei says, then laughs. Scott is blindfolded and gagged. The almost total darkness of the van blinds me; the smell is overwhelming.

"Scott, it's Cassandra," I say. I think I hear a sound, but it is hard to tell. There are two gags in Scott's mouth. One is soaked with blood. There's an overturned white milk crate next to the place where he lies. It is full of bloody dental tools and even bloodier gauze pads.

"Let him go!" My scream elicits a muffled gurgling sound from Scott.

"Shut up!" Alexei shouts, but Scott won't obey. Alexei turns and jabs one of the sharp silver tools through the gauze into Scott's mouth. Scott muffles a scream, but I wonder if he has any tears left. I wonder that about Samantha too. She's waiting for me outside, down by the lake. I wonder if she's still crying, or if she's smiling after learning she was right all along. There are creatures like me that live between the land of fact and faith. "I told you to shut up," Alexei says over Scott's muffled scream.

"Is he hurt?" I ask. The answer comes in the form of a bloody tooth landing at my feet.

"He's human," Alexei says, then laughs. "He's afraid and in pain. That's how we live."

Scott's making grunting sounds as he struggles to free himself from the handcuffs that anchor him down. His wrists seem as bloody as the area around his mouth.

"This isn't our way," I remind him, but Alexei laughs again.

"This is *my way*," he counters. "Should I take another one?"

"We live off the suffering of human beings, but we may not cause that suffering."

"Don't act like your hands are clean," he says. "Scott told me plenty about you, but then again, he didn't have a choice.

Since he wouldn't open his mouth to speak, I had to help him."

I try not to look at the tooth lying in front of me as I say, "I never did anything like this."

"You did plenty," he says. "We say we don't cause human suffering, but we all do!"

"No, it is not true!" I scream at him; I scream at myself. I scream for Robyn's soul.

"My way is more efficient, effective, if somewhat crude and bloody."

"Your way will reveal us!" I say, even though I've revealed too much to Samantha.

"It hasn't happened yet," he says, then reaches and grabs hold of my arm. "Maybe if I had a partner it would be easier."

"I don't want you to touch me!" I get my arm free, but only because he let go.

"You think that matters?" he hisses back. "You think any of us get what we want living among human beings, but never being part of them?"

"You can become one," I say, almost in a whisper. "Siobhan did, and I—"

"No, you can't. You're starting to feel human emotions, but that doesn't make you human. An ape can cry, a rat can laugh, but that doesn't make them human!"

"You don't know anything about me."

"I don't need to," he says. "You're just the soil for my seed."

"I won't do it," I counter. I hear Scott struggle again. I know I'm just as handcuffed and alone as he is. My family would be of no help. It is always about my obligation to them, never theirs to me. If I asked Mom, she would have to choose between generations. And I would lose.

"You don't have a choice," Alexei says, moving closer. From his feasting on Scott's tears, I know that he's stronger than ever. I can't defeat him in a struggle; I must surrender.

"Here's the deal. You let him go, and I'll let you walk out of here," I say, trying to sound as calm as possible. "We'll forget this ever happened."

"No, the deal is, you give yourself to me as promised," Alexei says almost upon me, "and I'll let him go."

"I don't believe you," is all I can say. "Let him go now."

"Don't worry, he's blindfolded. He won't see anything," Alexei says, then laughs.

"I'm begging you, let him go," I say, then actually drop to my knees.

Alexei towers over Scott, then asks me, "You want his suffering to end?"

"Yes. Please, let him go," I mutter, trying not to look at Alexei's ice blue eyes.

"Do you love him?" Alexei's hand is on the top of Scott's head.

"Just stop!"

"I'll stop *everything*," he says, then reaches over to Scott's

face, but he doesn't take the blindfold from his eyes or gag
from his mouth. Alexei puts one hand on Scott's nose, pinch-
ing it shut; the other hand covers his mouth. Scott's no swimmer; he's gasping for breath in seconds.

"Damn you!" I can't make myself move as Alexei clamps
down harder. There are so many rules in my family, but the
highest of all is "Do no harm" to human beings or your own
kind. If you must choose, then you choose family. To choose
the other is to choose exile.

"So which is it?" Alexei says as more seconds pass. Scott's
face turns blue and his wildly kicking feet stop. "He lives, if
you come to me. If you reject me, he dies. Choose."

"Damn you!" I shout again and take a step forward. I
can tell how strong Alexei is from feeding on Scott. I understand how weak I've become despite the energy Samantha
transferred to me through her tears. I must do what I've
been trained to do all my life: sacrifice myself. But unlike every
other time before, when I've sacrificed out of family obligation,
this is an act of selfishness. I'm giving myself up, so I can take
something for myself: Scott. I will die a little inside so that
Scott may live.

"You win, but not here. Outside," I say through clenched
teeth, then move toward the door. As I open the door, moonlight pierces the darkness. I glance back at Scott; he seems to
be barely breathing. He can't speak, but I hear his voice from
our first date: brains win wars. I need to think fast.

"Outside is perfect," Alexei says, then laughs as he steps away from Scott toward me.

I bolt from the door, and sprint from the van. I see Samantha far away by the lake; I see her car maybe twenty feet away. I dive into the night with all my speed as Alexei follows.

"Cassandra?" Alexei shouts after me. I was too quick for him. It starts as a question, but by the third time he yells my name into the darkness, it is a command. "Cassandra!"

Three more times he shouts my name into the darkness; the sixth time he shouts, it is over the roaring sound of Samantha's car as I push the gas pedal all the way to the floor. In seconds, I'm close enough to see the look of surprise in his eyes. He starts to yell, but he can't be heard over the sick sound of the car crashing into his human form.

"Scott, can you hear me?"

I check for a pulse; it is faint, and fading.

I take the bloody gag from his mouth. It looks like his front teeth are intact, although his gums are bleeding. I can't begin to imagine the ordeal he's endured, just like those abducted boys before him. I remove the black blindfold to see his nearly lifeless eyes. Tossing the dark rag onto the floor, I press the gauze against my shoulder. In seconds, it's as if a large ocean wave washes energy over me as remnants of Scott's terror absorbs into my skin. Once I feel reenergized, I reach into my back pocket and press the still-moist gauze into my—I mean

Veronica's—handkerchief and I start to pray that miracles still happen in the modern age.

I go to the front of the van and, for once, appreciate Alexei's arrogance. The keys remain in the ignition. From the key chain hangs one small key. I remove that key and seconds later remove the handcuffs from Scott's swollen wrists. He collapses face-first, eyes closed. I check his pulse again. It's weak; he's alive but failing fast. I open the door and yell for Samantha.

I know there is no time; there is only one choice. I open my phone and dial.

"Mom, I need your help," I say the second she answers the phone. I briefly explain Scott's status; I mention nothing of Samantha, or the carnage outside. "Scott needs *a* life."

"I can't do it," is her reply.

"But Veronica can," I say, but the words disappear into a cave of silence.

As I await an answer, I hear the van door open. Samantha stands there looking shocked. Before I can say anything, I hear her gasp.

"Scott, what happened?" she says, then crawls over toward him. She cradles his head in her lap, then starts crying. If only Scott were one of us, then Samantha's fresh and frantic tears would be enough to revive him. But he's not, so I await my mother's answer.

"Is he alive?" Samantha asks.

"Barely."

"We need to do something!" Samantha yells.

"I am doing something!" I shout back.

"We need to get him to a hospital. We need to—"

But I silence her when Mom comes back on the line. "Cassandra, you know that we can't do something like this."

"You *can* do it," I reply. "You're saying you *won't* do it."

"We will not, except in extreme cases," she counters.

"This *is* extreme!" I shout. "It is life or death."

She doesn't respond.

"I have collected human tears for Veronica as she's moved us around, always looking for more tragedy, more trauma," I say as words topple over one another. "I've done everything you've asked, and this is all I've ever asked of you in return. Save Scott's life!"

Mom pauses again, sighs, then says, "But you know how it works."

"Yes, I do," I say, then whisper so Samantha can't hear. "You know who to use."

"What you are asking—," she starts, but I cut her off.

"I'm asking for Veronica to sacrifice for me! I'm asking for someone to help me!"

Another pause. A pause lasting a lifetime of lifetimes. A pause ticking away the precious minutes of Scott's existence. The only sound in the world is my mom's silence.

"Mom, there's no more time. He's almost dead!" I shout over Samantha's crying.

"Cassandra, I'm sorry but—"

"If you don't do this for me," I say, "then you won't call me Cassandra again."

"What will I call you?" she asks.

I pause, sigh, and imagine the impact on her face. "You can call me Siobhan."

More silence on her end of the phone; more crying from Samantha in the background.

"We'll meet you there," Mom says.

"Thank you, thank you," I reply.

"Don't thank me. You will need to thank Veronica," she says.

"I will. I'm so—"

Mom cuts me off with words that sting like the end of a lash: "Then you'll owe her."

"I know," I say. "We're on our way."

I click the phone, then turn to Samantha. "We have to go."

"Which hospital?" she asks.

I crawl over to help her as we pull Scott out of the van.

"We're not going to a hospital."

"Then where are we going?" she asks, sounding angry and confused.

"To Avalon."

Samantha shakes her head in disbelief, and I say only, "You can trust me."

We're strong, but it's hard moving Scott's dead—or nearly dead—weight. It's a struggle, but we pull him out of the crashed van and into Samantha's car a few feet away. I don't see Alexei's body anywhere.

When we arrive at Avalon Convalescence Care, Mom's SUV is waiting for us in the employee parking lot in back. Other than Mom's car, there are only two other vehicles.

Maggie greets me as Samantha and I exit her car. Mom stands to the side.

"Who is that?" Maggie asks, pointing at Samantha, who looks scared.

"A *friend*," I reply, thinking how inadequate that word sounds now.

"If she's not family," Maggie whispers, "she stays behind."

"Don't you think Veronica will need her?" I whisper back.

Maggie ponders the questions, then says, "She can't know."

"She doesn't understand, I'll keep it that way," I lie directly to Maggie's face.

"You are drowning," Mom says. "You are in too—"

"Not now!" I cut her off. "Scott needs her help!"

Maggie nods, then heads inside. Mom goes to the car with me but refuses to make eye contact with Samantha.

Mom checks Scott's pulse, then shakes her head. "He might be too far gone."

"No!" I shout.

Maggie emerges from the employees-only door pushing two wheelchairs. She leaves one near Mom's SUV, then brings the other one to Samantha's car.

"We need your help," Maggie says to Samantha.

The four of us move Scott's limp body from the front of Samantha's car into the wheelchair. Mom and Maggie move quickly back to the car while I get behind the chair and start to push it up the ramp.

Samantha grabs my hand and asks, "What's happening?"

"I can't explain now," I say, softly.

"Will he be okay?"

"Maybe, but he'll need your help."

"What else can I do?" Samantha asks, eager to help, but unsure of what will be asked.

I turn, then point at Mom's car. Maggie and Mom are helping Veronica into the second wheelchair. She looks weak, too weak for what I'm asking her to do. "You need to go to the woman in the wheelchair. She needs you."

"Who is that?"

"That's the matriarch of our family, Veronica."

"I don't understand," Samantha mutters.

"You're not supposed to. Don't say anything," I say. "Go to her. She needs your energy."

"Energy?"

"Give her every tear left in your body," I say, then hug

her as if to force every ounce of liquid in her body toward her eyes. I hand her the folded-up paper with her poem, then say, "Show her that you hurt, hurt, hurt. Scott's life depends on it." Samantha leaves me, and I push Scott up the ramp.

Most of the lights are out as I push Scott through the deserted halls. Maggie meets me just short of our destination.

"There are only a few people on staff tonight," she says. "I told them I had some paperwork I needed to finish. They'll leave us alone."

"Where's Veronica?" I ask in desperation.

Maggie leans forward, then takes Scott's pulse again. "You're right, we need her now."

I hear the click of Maggie's shoes against the floor almost in time with the beeping of the machines. I push Scott inside the room. He's still not moving, but then again, neither is his grandmother. Machines keep her alive, but now it's only Veronica who can keep Scott among the living. Both Scott's and his grandmother's bodies are at rest; the inertia needs to be changed.

Mom pushes Veronica into the room minutes later. Her short time with Samantha must have been well spent. Even in the near darkness of the hall, she's almost glowing with energy.

"This is for you," I say to her, handing her the handkerchief monogrammed with her initials. Wrapped inside it is the gauze with Scott's tears. Veronica removes a vial from her jacket and sets it on the table next to Scott's grandmother's bed. The room's mostly dark, except for the light of the life-giving machines. Maggie sets a bowl on the table, then Veronica fills it with the contents from the vial. Mom steps in and takes the gauze from Veronica's hand. She dips it in the bowl, then puts the cloth on Veronica's face. It covers her face as if she's wearing a veil.

Filled with energy from Samantha and Scott, Veronica lifts herself out of the wheelchair and says, "You all must leave."

Before I can say anything, Veronica removes the cloth from her face and lets it rest on her shoulder. Her bright eyes stare through me, then she shuts the door behind us.

Moments that seem like hours later, we hear a holy trinity of sounds: a deep breath probably from Scott, a thud most likely from Veronica collapsing back into the wheelchair, and a last gasp from Scott's grandmother. One second later, the only noise is the flatlining beep from the monitor next to Scott's grandmother's bed. Mom opens the door and quickly grabs Veronica's wheelchair. Mom wheels Veronica past Maggie and me as we rush into the room.

I see Scott is breathing, but his grandmother's heart isn't beating. Veronica soaked up the energy in one life and transferred it to another. I grab Scott's wheelchair and head for the exit. He's barely conscious, but tries to speak. His words are garbled from the pain in his mouth, the blood in his throat, and the air reentering his lungs.

"Scott, are you okay?" I ask once we're outside. He still can't talk, but his eyelids flutter. I hold him tightly, not to capture his tears, but so I can hear the beat of his heart. I wonder if he can hear my heart. My almost-human heart.

*A*re you coming with us or not?"

Mom's reply is the same reply I've received from her since Scott's grandmother's death. Total silence. I'm emerging from my bedroom, my mood somber from the news I've seen on the computer this morning and the day stretched out before me. It will be odd to go to a funeral and sit in the pews rather than assisting at the altar, but everything will be odd from now on.

"You should come," I say to Mom. "Maggie's coming with me."

"I have nothing to say to you," she finally says.

"I'm sorry for what I've done, but I didn't have any choice," I reply, thinking about the choices I might have to make if I decide to follow Siobhan's example. Mom answers with a hard stare.

I escape Mom's disapproving eyes and head downstairs, where Maggie is waiting for me. We're both wearing black dresses befitting our place in the generations.

"What does he know?" Maggie asks as we leave the house. "What does the girl know?"

"She doesn't know anything," I lie to her. I've protected my family and our way of life for so long through silence. I will do the same now to protect my friends. Samantha will need to know that silence is her only protection. "And Scott doesn't remember anything."

"You're sure?" she asks.

"That's what he told me," I relate. I've only talked with Scott briefly, but learned that much from him. Today, after his grandmother's funeral, I'll try to find out more. But I know from peer counseling training how trauma destroys timelines and connections. Whatever part of Scott's brain tries to recall, the other half—the stronger half bent on survival—will suffocate.

"And that girl?" Maggie continues as we walk to the car. "Samantha, right?"

"Samantha's a joke. She thinks monsters are real," I say, then fake a laugh. "Even if she knows something, no one would believe her. She's the girl who cried werewolf."

"What about you?" she asks.

"What about me?"

"All of this—the miracle you witnessed in the nursing home, whatever happened or didn't happen with Alexei—all of it," Maggie says, almost accusingly. "What about you?"

"I'm the same," I mumble. I remember reading somewhere the bigger the lie, the more likely people are to believe it.

"Cassandra, I don't believe you," she says.

"I don't know what else to tell you," I say, then sigh.

"You're not the same," she says. "And you haven't been for a long time."

"You're wrong," I say as we climb into the car.

"No, Cassandra, I'm right. You can deny it, but I know. I've known it for a while."

"What do you mean?" I ask.

"I knew you were changing," she says. "Ever since that day you got so mad at us."

"You mean every day," I say, and let out a small laugh. She doesn't respond.

"The day you said you made all the sacrifices," she says. "I guess you were wrong."

I pause for a second, thinking how no action is without impact. "How is Veronica?" I ask.

"She's already started to rebuild her strength," she says. "She's so *damn strong*."

"I didn't know it would take so much out of her," I say slowly because Maggie's tone seems wrong, as does her choice of words. The angry hard look on her face tells even more.

"Maggie, you seem so angry," I say. "What is going on?"

"I'll set a good example and be honest with you. It's time you know anyway," she says.

"Time I know?"

"It is my turn to be matriarch instead of Veronica," she says. "Just as it is your turn to be with Alexei."

"I don't understand," I say. As part of the youngest genera-tion, I know I've been kept in the dark about many rules of our lives. The more rules I learn, the more I have to fight against.

"It is time for my mother to go, so I can take over as the head of the family," Maggie says. We're sitting in a modern car talking about the ancient ways. "But she refuses to go."

"And then what happens to me?" I ask.

"Then you bring in the next generation, and you become the mother in the family," she continues. "Do you understand now why Veronica wasn't angrier with you about Alexei?"

"What do you mean?" I ask as I ponder Veronica's anger, that now seemed all an act.

"If you don't mate, then the next generation doesn't begin," she continues. "And she can stay on, even if it is supposed to be my time. Cassandra, you're not the selfish one, Veronica is."

"I'm not ready."

"It doesn't matter. It is our nature," she says, as she backs out of the driveway.

I sink into myself. I can't tell her the truth. I can't tell her that I'm learning to defy my nature. She can't know that I feel love and that I want to feast on happiness, not sadness.

"A lot has happened these past few days, Cassandra, but your family is always going to be there for you," she says softly. "And you need to be there for them, no matter what."

"I know," I say, but without any conviction.

"So, Cassandra, are you still one of us, or have you become one of *them*?" she asks.

I never speak out at school unless I am one hundred percent sure of the answer. Maggie and I drive to Saint Dominic's in total silence.

Scott looks to have regained some strength as he, along with other men from Saint Dominic's Church, carry his grandmother's casket up the aisle. I'd like to sit with him, but death, like life, is about family. I sit with Maggie. Samantha is next to me; she holds her notebook in one hand and the other presses a tissue against her cheek. For once, being dressed head-to-toe in black is appropriate and accepted. As the church fills with tears, every cell in me seeks them out. Samantha seems to have overcome her inability to express emotion by allowing herself to cry in public. I fight off the urge to touch her. I still don't know if I can provide real comfort. All my life, I've only pretended compassion when what I really did was consume.

The service goes on for a long time, as several members from Saint Dominic's speak in addition to Father Morrison. All of them talk about what a giving person Scott's grandmother was, and I can't help but think about my family: who gives, who takes, and what is owed. Veronica has said nothing to me since the incident, mainly because she lacks the energy to speak. Mom attends to her every day, and for that reason alone, I'm surprised she's not mixing in among the mourners to take her share of energy. Once again, it falls to me to serve Veronica.

"Death is the far-right bookend," Scott says when it is his turn to speak. He looks uncomfortable in his black suit; his words are barely understandable through his obviously still painful mouth. He speaks slowly yet softly, as if the gauze were still in him soaking up his blood. Alexei tortured him with those dental tools—jabbing at gums, pulling teeth, anything to cause fear and pain in order to produce tears. Scott's mouth will heal; that trauma will linger.

"And my grandmother's life, like every life, was filled with stories," Scott says, then tells stories about his grandmother's life. The microphone bounces his words off the stained-glass images of saints and martyrs. I try to pay attention, but my thoughts are elsewhere, yet also right above me. At Saint Dominic's, our family sits on the left side, underneath the stained-glass Stations of the Cross. We always sit under station six: Veronica wipes Jesus' face with her veil. Just as Alexei's family would normally sit under the fifth station: Simon carries Jesus' cross.

"The sad thing in death is knowing there are no more stories to create. There are only stories to tell. As long as a person remains alive in story, they remain alive in spirit," Scott says, then his eyes look out over the crowded church. He pauses, then finds me in the crowd. "So, tell stories of your own family. If you do this, then each family lives longer than their time on earth."

"Your speech was nice," I tell Scott as I slip next to him in the receiving line. I sat with Maggie in church, but I'm standing with Scott as people prepare to walk past to pay their respects to him. This, more than the upcoming prom, bestows official girlfriend status on me.

"Thanks," he whispers, then pulls me closer to him.

"I'm so sorry, Scott," I say.

"It was time."

"Not just about your grandmother, but about the other thing," I say softly.

He looks away from me; I don't blame him.

"Alexei is my cousin. Like I told you, he's insane," I explain. "He stole my phone. Nothing happened between us. There's no one but you, Scott."

"I believe you, Cass," he says, then starts to cry. As I touch one of Scott's tears, I know instantly everything is all right between us. I've learned that every tear, just like every grain of sand, has a different texture. But tears of any kind now rip me apart.

"Please don't cry," I say. I've never said these three words together before. Scott can never know that my saying "please don't cry" is proof that the words "I love you" are true.

Scott takes a deep breath and pulls himself together. "Are you okay?" I ask.

He tries to smile, but can't. Instead, he says, "That's the only thing I really remember clearly."

"What?"

"Your voice asking me if I was okay," he whispers. "And I knew, because it was your voice, everything would be okay."

"You don't remember anything else?" I ask as I take hold of his hand.

"Nothing else that matters," he says, then kisses me on the cheek. His mom clears her throat and the mourners start to file past. And in a way, I'm mourning too. Not for Scott's grandmother but for myself—what I was and what I hope to become. I'm not there yet. Once again I find myself in between. So while I stand in this line for Scott and offer compassionate embraces to all the grieving relatives, I must still be here for my own family. I owe them.

After the last person passes by, we all gather outside next to the hearse. Scott joins the other men from the church lifting the white coffin into the black vehicle. Before he gets into the limo that will lead the procession to the cemetery, I go up to him and give him another kiss. Then I wipe away his tears with the soft gentleness of my hand instead of the coarseness and calculation of my monogrammed handkerchief. I wipe away his tears, not for me or for Veronica, but for him.

As the hearse starts off toward the cemetery, I head back

to Maggie's car, where together we start the drive in silence. As we pull into the funeral possession behind a long line of limos, Maggie finally speaks. "You didn't answer my question. I saw you with Scott. Are you still—?"

"I didn't answer because I don't know."

"Cassandra, I know this is hard for you. It was for me, and your mother," Maggie says as we drive slowly to the cemetery. "But you have a duty to your family."

"Why Alexei?" I ask. No one in the family seems to know where he is. I still don't know if I should tell the family the things that he did to Scott and to those young boys. Everyone is looking for Alexei, but I hope they never find him. I must not have hit him hard enough with the car, or maybe he was too strong from soaking up so many of Scott's tears, but I know from the news alert I printed this morning that he is still out there, hiding in the dark shadows.

"Because that's how it is. After, you'll come back home just as your mother and I did," she says. "You need to mate to create the next generation. Cassandra, it is your turn."

"Why does it have to be me?" I watch the limos in front snake down the streets of Lapeer.

"For the same reason the sun rises in the morning: because it is how the world works," Maggie says. "Our family is part of the natural order. These are the rules of our lives."

"I hate these rules!" I shout, like a child throwing a tantrum. "I hate Alexei. I love Scott!"

"Cassandra, you don't love Scott," she says. Her lips move, but I try to block out her words. "You think you love him, but you don't. In fact, you can't. That is not who we are."

I say nothing because I cannot speak the truth. I want to tell her that I've proven my love for Scott, that I can cry and feel like a human. As soon as I learn Siobhan's secret, I will leave Maggie, Veronica, and Mom behind. But I can't say this yet. Not yet.

"This is how we live," she says. "The males stay separate and come to us only to prolong the species. It is not about love or any of those human emotions. It is about our survival."

"But Siobhan—," I start.

Maggie cuts me off with a glare. "Don't speak her name. She is a traitor to her kind," she says. "She betrayed her family. She betrayed her values. There is a natural order to things, and when she left this family, she selfishly disturbed that order."

"She was in love," I counter with the most defiant tone I can muster.

"It's *impossible* for us to feel that way," she continues. "Love is a human illusion."

I want to tell her how wrong she is. Love isn't an illusion, but it might be magic.

"Siobhan isn't selfish," I say, thinking of all the selfish people I know, like Brittney.

"Cassandra, listen to me," she says as she pulls the car over. "Everybody in the family has had these doubts. Do you think you're the first? We live among humans; it is natural that we should want to be like them. Being like them not just in appearance but by feeling emotions—the very thing that makes them human. But we can't feel emotions because they would drain us, and then we couldn't fulfill our place in nature. The family would cease to exist. It's science, not supernatural. Don't blame me, your mom, or Veronica; blame evolution."

"But Siobhan—," I try again, but once more, she cuts me off.

"Siobhan has nothing. She is an orphan, an exile, an outsider. I don't want that for you. Is that what you want?" she asks, and I respond with a strange look. Is this some odd bonding attempt or some trick? As obligation replaces emotion in my family, every motive is suspect.

"I want Scott," I answer.

"How long have you known him?" she asks. "Something like two weeks?"

"Almost two months," I say. "He means everything to me."

"If you leave the family, then you can't come back," she says.

She looks at me like no family member has ever looked at me before. Even if it is just an act, it still means something. I know she can't feel it, but she can fake it; it is a loving look of worry and concern. "Cassandra, if you lose your family," she says, "then, you lose *everything*."

· · ·

After the service and the funeral repast, Scott, Samantha, and I are sitting outside of the Family Center. He's loosened his tie, while Samantha has removed the black headband wrapped around her head. She dabs her eyes with it, winks, then hands it to me like a secret handshake.

"What are you doing?" Scott asks.

Samantha pauses, then looks over at me. I owe her Scott's life; she owes me her silence. I stare back at Scott, then say, "What do you think she's doing?"

"I don't know," he says, then shrugs. "I'm saying that a lot these days."

"You don't remember any of it?" Samantha asks. This is the first time she's seen Scott since everything happened. She doesn't see my eyes, pleading with her to shut up.

"I remember visiting my grandmother after you left on Saturday morning," Scott says. Depending on what else he remembers, some details might be hard to explain away even to a person who says he believes in the supernatural. He told me once that he believes in angels and thus must believe in demons. I wonder if he can believe in creatures that are not evil but live off human suffering. "I remember getting your text, Cass, and then going to meet you."

"Then what?" I ask. Scott doesn't need to know it was Alexei, not me, texting him.

"I wanted to see you so badly," he says. "So, I went to meet you at the little park near the nursing home. And then . . ."

He falls silent again, and I wait. Details may return and one day he'll know the truth, but maybe by then, he will be as in love with me as I am with him and none of this will matter.

"Then I woke up in my own bed on Monday morning," he says. "I woke up with my mouth in terrible pain and two back teeth missing. I woke up to the news that my grandmother had died. But in between, I don't recall anything, other than your voice asking me if I was okay."

"That must have been just a dream," I say. Better he think that than know the real nightmare.

"No, it was more like I was in a coma," he says. "I just don't know what happened. My mom called the police, but they told her that there's not much they can do."

"They search for missing persons, not missing days out of a person's life," Samantha says. She knows the truth, but she's proving her trustworthiness with her silence.

"If Mom could afford it, I bet she'd hire a private detective," Scott says.

"Maybe you were in a car accident or got mugged," Samantha says, practicing her fiction-writing skills. "Maybe you were abducted by aliens who conducted all sorts of—"

"In that case," Scott says, trying to smile, "maybe it's better I don't remember!"

"Sounds like a plan," I say.

"Once this all dies down, my mom wants me to see somebody," he continues.

"What do you mean?" I ask, trying to keep Scott talking and testing the limits of his memory. While we're talking, Samantha is writing in her notebook. I shoot her a dirty look.

"She wants me to see a therapist to help with all this trauma," he says.

Samantha chimes in. "I've got something else you might want to consider as well."

"What's that?" Scott asks.

"I'd also recommend the peer counseling program at Lapeer High School," she says, and both of us laugh. Scott tries to, but ends up coughing instead. He takes a tissue from his coat pocket and puts it up to his mouth. When he removes it, it's stained with blood.

"Are you in pain?" Samantha asks. I guess Scott answers, but I'm not listening. Instead, I'm thinking about all the suffering and sorrow that Scott, Samantha, Becca, Becca's parents, and every human experience, and how it benefits me. And how I want it still.

I wish I could retrieve all the tissues from inside the church and harvest all the tears cried during the service. I took in a lot of emotion from strangers during the service, but I need more. When I get back to school, I'll need to spread new rumors and stir up drama. When I get back to the hospital, I'll need to comfort as many crying families as I can. When I get back to Becca, I'll make her feel better for as long as she lives by letting her cry in front of me. And then, then I'll take the tears home to Veronica who has grown weak; I'll need to be strong for her. I will need to thrive on people as I feed on their sadness. I will have to continue to collect tears until I'm able to reject this way of living. Until that day, which I sense is coming sooner than later, I'm still dwelling on the threshold.

"I need to say good-bye to people," I hear Scott say, then he kisses me very lightly on the cheek. This morning he said one of the hardest good-byes of his life; any other has to be easy.

"I'll see you later," I say as I push his perfectly combed hair out of his face, kiss him on the forehead, and then watch him blush. It's nice to see some color back in his face.

Once Scott is out of sight, Samantha turns to me and says, "Thanks, Cass."

"For what?"

"For saving Scott's life," she says.

"That wasn't me," I counter. "That was Veronica, but mostly it was you."

"Me?"

"You gave her the strength," I whisper. "By showing your emotions you helped Scott. He's still in pain, so he needs your support. You're so mature, Samantha. Most girls—"

"Most girls didn't come from families as screwed up as mine," she says, still holding back tears. "You get really mature, really fast, when you have to raise yourself."

"I wouldn't know about that," I say. "I'm just glad we can all be friends."

"I need to know," Samantha says after I pause. "I don't understand so much of what—"

But I cut her off, then take her hand and say, "You can *never* understand. You can *never* tell anyone, and I can't tell you more than you've seen. You have to promise me this."

"I promise, Cass," she says.

"Listen, if you break the promise, then you'll learn how far we're willing to go to protect our secret."

She nods, accepting the threat, but says, "There's so much I want to know. So much that—"

"Trust me, it is better for you if you don't know too much," I say.

"Can you just tell me what happened in the nursing home? How did Scott end up alive and his grandmother dead?" she asks, but I don't answer. "Just explain that part to me."

"I can't explain it," I say. "Like most things in life, truth rests between faith and facts."

"Can I ask one last question?" she says. "You owe me that much. What are you really?"

I pause, then say, "We call ourselves the Family. We're like an emotional succubus or what you'd call an energy vampire," I say, trying to explain the unexplainable. "But we're not monsters. We don't have superpowers all the time, but we can, when filled with tears, act with great strength and energy. Mostly, we're like every other species on this planet that has adapted to survive. Despite what you saw from Alexei, most of us are not

NEWS REPORT #6

Illinois State Police have issued an AMBER Alert for thirteen-year-old Barry Wilson. Wilson, a seventh-grade student at North Chicago Middle School, was last seen on April 17. Witnesses place him in the playground of the school where he was playing baseball with friends. After a disagreement during the game, Wilson left the playground alone. One witness said he was crying. Law enforcement officials are on the lookout for a black Ford van seen in the area earlier in the day.

evil, and we do our best to live among humans without directly causing pain, both to avoid detection and because it is wrong."

"But for you to survive, humans must suffer," she says.

"Humans already suffer. We just soak up that energy. If we didn't serve a purpose on this earth," I remind her, "we wouldn't survive."

"I wish I could write about all this. Don't you think this could be a book?" She looks at her notebook, then back at me. "Cass, if I could write about all of this, then how do you think such a book should start?"

I take a sip from my water bottle, smile at Samantha, and then say, "Are you crying?"

CHAPTER 19

MONDAY, APRIL 20

How was my spring break?" I say, repeating Mr. Abraham's question to me. We're sitting near the edge of the pool. It's after school, and I'm waiting for Scott to come pick me up. He missed school today, and I missed him. Like a detective piecing together the clues to a crime, this new feeling of missing Scott is another sign that Maggie is wrong: love isn't just an illusion; it's my new reality.

"All right, I guess," I say, my feet dangling in the water, just like my answer barely touches the truth. How was my spring break? Busy, I guess. In a few days, I helped save one life, but in doing so, took another. I saw a person I love tortured and I was almost raped. I learned secrets about my family, while revealing my deepest secret to a person that I don't even know I can totally trust. It wasn't a break; it was a rip in the fabric of my life. "What did you do, Mr. A?"

"Nothing exciting," he says, and I try not to laugh almost

as hard as I try to listen, but my mind is drifting. He catches me and asks, "Are you listening?"

"I always listen," I mutter, mainly to myself.

"That's what makes you such a good peer counselor," he says.

I swallow the smile that comes with a compliment, then mumble, "I need to quit."

"What? Peer counseling?"

"It's too hard to listen to people's problems," I answer. In the past, I soaked up people's pain and tears like a sponge, but I know, deep inside of me, that I can't do it anymore. Like an alcoholic avoiding bars and parties, I need to avoid opportunities to get my grief fix. If the first step was realizing I have a choice, then the second, I assume, is deciding to live without tears. I need to wean myself off tears for when I convince Siobhan to reveal the third and final step into humanity.

"You're so good at it, and we need you. Many students are still in pain over Robyn," he says. I think not about school, but Robyn's family. I must see them all, not for me, but for them.

"I know," I say, then fall deep into thought. Mr. Abraham's still talking, but I've diverted my attention and my eyes to the pool.

"Maybe *you* need to talk to someone," Mr. Abraham says with a nervous chuckle.

"What do you mean?"

"You seem distracted," he says.

"Can I ask you something?" I ask, as if each word weighs a hundred pounds.

"Of course, Cassandra," he answers.

"How do you know what to do?" I'm back to staring at the pool.

He laughs first, but then smiles. His expression is familiar to me not from life, but from TV and movies. It's that concerned and caring look a daughter hopes to see in their father's eyes.

"Sorry, that was a stupid question," I say.

"There are no stupid questions," he says. "Just questions that are badly phrased. What did you mean, Cassandra, when you asked that question? Do about what?"

"I mean, how do you make an important decision?" But even as he looks within himself for an answer, I realize my question itself is the answer. All my life, my family has lived like animals: we survive as a pack. Like a wild creature cares only about finding prey and nourishment, so, too, does my family only act out of animal instinct. We don't really decide anything, for making a decision is a human activity.

When Mr. A can tell I'm paying attention again, he starts. "What I'm about to say isn't very helpful, but *you just know*. For all we talk in science about evidence, trial and error, and all the rigors of the scientific method, sometimes you just know. You don't listen to your head or your heart. There's something in between that must hold the answer. Don't listen to science;

instead, listen to the silence. And in that silence, answers and inspiration always emerge."

"Like a message from God?"

He shrugs, then says, "No, Cassandra, more like a message from your true self."

I get dressed and wait for Scott by the front door of the school. I don't know about listening to the silence; instead, I decide to listen to Siobhan. She always says she won't talk to me, then she always does. When compassion isn't just an act, it is much harder to turn off, I suppose. I reach out to her new humanity on my cell phone.

"Hello, Siobhan, it's Cassandra. How are you—?"

"I heard."

"Heard?"

"You're not the only cousin I talk to," she says, sounding a little impatient. "Like I've told you before, you need to leave me out of this. I've left the family. That's all in the past."

"What did you hear?" I ask, pretending that I didn't hear her little speech.

"About you rejecting Alexei," she says. "Do you realize what you've done?"

"Yes."

"What do you think is going to happen?" she asks.

"I don't know."

"I'll tell you, cousin, so you do know," she says. The

impatient tone in her voice returns. "Simon won't stand for this, nor will Veronica. Alexei will be back. You don't have a choice."

"But I do," I say. "You told me I had a choice. I believed you. I've made my choice."

She pauses, then sighs. "This is serious. You can't undo it. This is forever."

"I know," I say, thinking how Maggie said something similar. "But, do you regret it?"

"To be honest, sometimes yes," she says. "I know you don't want to hear that, but, yes, I wonder sometimes if I did the right thing. Your family is forever, but human love doesn't always work out that way. I want you to understand this choice is a matter of life and death."

"Life and death?"

"If you leave, then who will collect tears for Veronica? You'll be breaking the chain."

"They'll survive somehow," I say. "Your family managed, didn't they?"

She pauses. "Yes, everyone pulled together, but it is so much more than just that. You're killing off your old self to gain a human life."

"But how?"

"How do you think it happens?" Siobhan asks. "To become human, you must . . . ," she continues. "Cass, you have to know what comes next."

"To become human, I must . . . I must take a human life."

"You drain all the human energy into your body," she says. "And then you are transformed."

"Are you saying that you killed—," I start, but it is a question I don't want to ask, one that I know she doesn't want to answer, and one that shows me whatever I thought the stakes were, they just got a great deal higher.

"Listen, Cassandra, I can't tell you what to do," she says, words racing out of her. "I'm telling you the risks, you already know the rewards. And I'm telling you the heavy, heavy cost."

"Who was it? Who did you kill?" I ask, but I'm left listening only to the silence.

"Siobhan?" She doesn't answer; she just hangs up.

I wanted to know how she did it, but now I wish I didn't. I knew it couldn't be as easy as just falling in love. I saved Scott's life, but to be like him and with him, I need to take away someone else's life. I don't know if I'm that strong. I'm not sure who is that weak.

"Does it still hurt?" I ask after pulling away from Scott's kiss. I climb into his car.

"A little," he says, then smiles. "But it makes it better. I'll need a daily dose of your kisses."

"Can we make a stop at Becca's on the way?" I ask. Scott and I are going out tonight to look at prom dresses. We're meeting Samantha at the store; she'll be going with her theater pal, Michael—a last minute fix-up, another high school relationship of convenience and coincidence.

"Anything for you," he says as we drive off toward the mall. "How was school today?"

"Interesting," I respond, smiling like I do all the time now, it seems. Smiling at Scott and at the Beatles music he has playing for me. But mostly smiling at how far short the word "interesting" falls when used to describe my life since the day in early March when I first saw Robyn crying in her car.

"I'll be back at school tomorrow, but you might want to skip," Scott says.

"Why's that?"

"It's not going to be pretty. I might be getting the crap beat out of me," Scott says, then actually laughs. "I mean my mouth is already broken, so I figure now seems as good a time as any to get my ass kicked. When you're already in pain, I say pile it on."

"What are you talking about?" I ask. "Who is going to kick your ass?"

"Probably Craig," he says.

"Why? What did you do?"

"It's what I'm going to do," he says with pride. "I'm going to tell his girlfriend Brittney off. If he's a man, he'll stand up for her. Not that she deserves it or will appreciate it."

"Why would you do that?" I hope he can hear the worry in my voice.

"I thought about the rumors, the lies she spread about you and Robyn," Scott says. "I know the Christian thing to do is forgive her, but I just can't. Her sins are unforgivable, at least by me. But it's not just the rumors. It's more than that. In fact, it is everything about her."

"I don't understand," I say. That's the last lie that I'll ever tell him, I promise myself.

"Everything I can't stand in a person is embodied in Brittney," he continues. "I know it is wrong to be so judgmental, but Brittney's shallowness, her lack of caring about others. It's all so wrong."

"That's not the worst of it," I start, and then I stoke the fires, telling Scott about Brittney spreading rumors and using people like Kelsey to do her dirty work. I remind him Brittney had Kelsey lie to him about me cheating on him with Craig. I tell him about her fake tears when Robyn died and her threat to me when I wouldn't take down Robyn's Facebook profile. I tell him about Brittney's role in Robyn's death. Maybe Robyn killed herself, but if she did, she didn't just jump—she was pushed, with Brittney's fingerprints all over her back. Just like my knife is in Brittney's back now.

"I think about her, your friend Becca, and wonder if maybe Samantha was right," he says.

"What do you mean, Scott?"

"Maybe there isn't a God. How could a just God let someone like my grandma or Robyn die, while people like Brittney don't just live, they seem to thrive."

As I watch Scott's face tighten, I realize I've gone too far, probably because it's a path that I'm so used to taking. "That was wrong. Don't say anything to her," I whisper. The old me was trained to stir up drama and trauma—and I still can't resist those impulses. Every day will be a struggle against my nature.

"No, it's like that night of our first date in the restaurant. You gotta stand up to people like this," Scott says. "If you get hit, you just turn the other cheek, but you don't turn a blind eye to bad behavior."

"Bullies like Brittney, they're not that strong," I say. "Deep down, I know she's weak."

"Yet another reason you don't let the Brittneys of the world win without fighting back."

"This is why I love you," I say. The words roll off my tongue easily now. It was much harder to say to Cody when I didn't mean it. That drained my energy, but saying "I love you" to Scott brings me more. My family finds energy in tears; humanity finds it in love. I wrap my arms around Scott as the sound of "Across the Universe" fades out. I let the silence surround me. There's no sound now except the beating of two hearts in perfect time.

"Becca's sleeping," Mrs. Berry tells me soon after Scott and I arrive at their house.

"I should have called first," I say, looking down.

"You never have to call," she says, opening the door wider, allowing Scott and me to enter. It's been a month since Robyn died, but nothing's changed. Pictures of Robyn hang on the walls. It's like they're still waiting for her to walk in the door. They're stuck on stage one: denial.

"This is my boyfriend, Scott," I say proudly, loving how those five words sound together.

"Any friend of Cassandra's is welcome here. Nice to meet you, Scott," Mrs. Berry says, then ushers us into the house. "John is still at work. He needs his work now more than ever."

"I understand," Scott says. And I know he does. Loss creates new connections.

"I'm not working right now," she volunteers as Scott and I sit down. "I'm spending as much time as I can at home with Becca. I want to cherish every minute that I have with her."

"How is she doing?" I ask. "I'm sorry I haven't been here more."

"It's been hard on her," Mrs. Berry says. "Her spirit is strong even if her body is growing weaker every day."

"How are *you* doing?" I ask, almost in a whisper. "Is there anything I can do?"

"It's not easy, Cassandra," she says, very slowly. "It was just such a shock. With Becca, we know what is coming, but that still doesn't make it any easier."

I lean closer. My hands reach out to her, not into my back pocket. I left Veronica's handkerchief at home. Whatever tears I take will be just enough to survive until I find strength to take a life and transform myself. Mrs. Berry pulls herself together, then says, "It's just so hard."

"Mrs. Berry, if it were easy, it wouldn't be love," I say to her, but I'm looking at Scott. I remember his words from that first time we talked, and I think about how they've come true. Yet, to feel fully human love, I know that I must still do something very hard to someone very weak.

Silence invades the room; memories of Robyn attack my mind. I feel like crying, which I've always wanted to do, but stop myself. Mrs. Berry doesn't need my tears and I don't want hers.

"Scott, come help me fix iced tea for the two of you," she says, then rises. "Cassandra, why don't you go look in on Becca. Maybe she's awake now. She'll want to see you."

"Sure thing," I say. Scott gives me a soft kiss on the cheek. He goes into the kitchen with Mrs. Berry, while I go upstairs. It's stupid, but with just a few feet and seconds between us, I feel a sense of separation from Scott. It proves we belong together, now and forever.

As I walk upstairs, it's as if each step is the beat of a drum. I want to be with Scott; I want to be a human. I want to live on love, not on tears. To be human, I must take a human life.

Becca's asleep, and my opening the door doesn't change that fact. Becca's near death, maybe six months to live, but I could open a door for myself and change that fact. Robyn wanted to trade her life for Becca, but it is not going to work out that way. Instead, Becca could trade what's left of her life for me. Within me, Becca could, in a sense, live on. I'd be honoring

Robyn, I'd be helping Becca, but mostly I'm just trying to convince myself.

My humanness grows deeper; even thinking about this action overwhelms me with guilt. The guilt is compounded by Becca's innocence and the purity of her brave struggle this past year and a half. A struggle she will not win; a struggle that I could end to solve my own problems.

I'm near her bed. Next to the bed on a table are the tools of a vibrant youth: a phone, a PSP, an iPod. On another table are the tools of sickness: pills, needles, medical gloves.

Downstairs I hear Scott talking to Mrs. Berry. It seems cruel to know that by the time they've moved somewhat past Robyn's death, the grieving will start all over again when they lose Becca. If she died now it would probably be more merciful.

As I stand next to her, my hands are shaking. Why did this innocent child have this disease inflicted upon her? There are so many guilty people in the world—people who are cruel, selfish, and uncaring—who get to live while this innocent child has to die.

Samantha said the unfairness of the world proves that there's no God. If the world became fair, would that prove there is a God? Or is fairness as random as fate?

All of these thoughts swim in my head, but they're crashing against each other. Every thought stands alone and against another. I close my eyes and listen to the silence.

I know what I must do to become human. Siobhan did it, and I must do it too.

This is what I want. This is what I need.

I know what I need to do to make it happen.

There is no turning back; there is only one road stretching before me.

But there will be guilt—guilt that feels worse staring into the sleeping face of this innocent dying child. I watch her sleep, breathe, dream—but mostly I just listen to the silence.

Finally, the answer emerges: to be transformed into a human, I cannot act inhumanely and steal the life force from someone I care so much about.

I stare at Becca sleeping. She looks more peaceful in sleep than she does awake.

Reaching over to the table, I make my move. I place the object in my hand. The weight of it feels right as I softly speak these words into the phone: "Hello, Brittney, it's Cassandra. I need to see you."